THE SCHOOL FROM HELL?

Here For A Year? Forget It!

Yvonne Coppard is British and lives in Cambridgeshire with her husband and two children. She works as an advisory teacher (child protection), and has written a number of books; the two listed below for Piccadilly Press have been well-reviewed and bestsellers:

Don't Let It Rain!
Great! You've Just Ruined the Rest of My Life

THE SCHOOL FROM HELL?

Here For A year? Forget It!

Yvonne Coppard

Piccadilly Press • London

for Annie Quirk, with love and kisses

Printed and bound in Bridgend, South Wales by WBC
for the publishers Piccadilly Press Ltd,
5 Castle Road, London NW1 8PR

A catalogue record for this book is available from the
British Library

ISBNs: 1 85340 412 8 (trade paperback)
1 85340 417 9 (hardback)

Cover design Dave Crook
Interior design by Judith Robertson

Chapter 1

*T*he school bus, freshly washed and polished to an impressive shine, pulled up at the station with a screech of brakes and a faint smell of burning rubber. This had little to do with the bus, which was only a year old. It was more to do with Manfred's enthusiasm for driving and 'testing that everything works before we take pupils aboard.' As Manfred explained to his two passengers, you could only properly test a motor by running it at high speed and then slamming on the brakes.

'But isn't that a bit dangerous?' Stephanie asked, as she watched the high brick wall of the station come into view. 'I mean, what if you find out the brakes don't work after all, just as you're doing one hundred kilometres an hour into a brick wall?'

Manfred smiled in his very superior way. 'Then we thank God we didn't have any children on board,' he said. And that was apparently that. As it happened, the bus did come to a halt before the brick wall (just) and so King Arthur's English Academy was spared having to find a new bus driver and replace two teachers right at the start of term.

Brandon Leddan (sports and leisure) and Stephanie Harvey (languages) descended from the bus looking very relieved to have survived the journey, and greeted Fred, the station master.

'Five minutes,' Fred grinned, looking at his watch. 'And then your holidays are over.'

'I just hope Letty managed to catch the train in London and stop them getting all wound up,' said Stephanie.

'If you wanted them to arrive here calm and collected, you

should be hoping she missed the train again this year,' grinned Fred.

Letty Domingo (arts and drama) was not known for her punctuality or her ability to control groups of pupils. But she had a wonderful smile, looked ravishing and was an artist of some repute. Charles Asquith, the headmaster, had appointed her in the hope that somewhere along the way she would also learn how to teach.

As the train trundled into Morton Gipping Station, Fred drew himself up to his full height and straightened his cap. Very few people came to Morton Gipping by train, except for the school folk; it had been a very slow summer. Now he looked forward to the constant traffic of pupils coming and going from the station, and he wanted to set the right tone and make sure everybody got the impression that he was not a man to be trifled with. Just because they came from rich and famous families, didn't mean they could mess Frederick Arthur Potter about.

Stephanie and Brandon exchanged nervous glances. 'Here goes,' said Stephanie.

The train doors opened and a mass of talking, chattering bodies clad in blue and black striped blazers were deposited on the station platform. There were about fifty of them on this train, with three more trains due in that day and another four the next morning. There was no sign of Letty, who had promised faithfully to come down on the first train and give a hand with settling people in. None of the other teachers would be arriving until the evening.

'Right,' called Brandon. 'New pupils over here with me, please. Everyone else on to the coach as quickly as you can. Thanks.'

The old hands pushed and shoved their way through to the carpark, where they exchanged affectionate insults with

Manfred, who was the school caretaker as well as the driver. (He also ran a little motorbike maintenance course on a Saturday morning, in return for the use of one of the garages where he and a few of the sixth-formers were 'doing up' an old Bentley.) As they passed through the station exit, Stephanie hauled back the new pupils who had misunderstood instructions and were following the crowd.

Charles Asquith, the headmaster of King Arthur's, was very proud of Stephanie, who had been the first teacher he appointed. She was not only strikingly attractive (which was a prime consideration when appointing staff for King Arthur's), but she could speak six languages and was also highly organised. Furthermore, she was actually a good teacher. Charles had not been able to believe his luck. A teacher like Stephanie could have worked anywhere, but she had wanted peace and isolation, as she intended to write a novel in her spare time. That was what she had told the interview panel, anyway. Charles suspected there was more to it than that, especially as no novel had appeared. But in five years he had never worked out what it could be.

Calmly, Stephanie pointed out to the pupils where to stand, what was happening, who she was etc, in whatever language worked. Then she went over to help Brandon identify who they all were, and tick them off the list.

Brandon was deeply engrossed in an attempted conversation with a smiling Chinese girl. 'What is your name?' he was asking very slowly. The girl smiled.

Stephanie asked the question again, in French. Then she tried Spanish, Portuguese, German and Dutch.

The girl's smile wavered uncertainly, and then returned. She waited patiently for them to say something she could understand.

'Sorry, I'm out of languages,' Stephanie told Brandon.

'They're supposed to pass a basic English test, aren't they?' groaned Brandon.

'Only if the Lunatic Lord doesn't particularly want them for his school,' said Stephanie, referring to the headmaster by his usual affectionate title with the staff. 'Her parents must be worth a fair bit.'

Brandon looked down his list. 'She has to be one of two people,' he said. 'Look, here are the Chinese names.'

'Chen See Lee?' asked Stephanie.

The girl smiled and nodded.

'Oh good. It had to be that or Han Pwee Lah.'

The girl nodded and smiled.

'Ah. Right. Are you Han Pwee Lah, then?' asked Brandon.

The girl nodded and bowed slightly.

'Or are you Chen See Lee?' asked Stephanie, suddenly suspicious.

The girl nodded and bowed again.

The smile was beginning to irritate Brandon. He looked at his clipboard, where he had the admission list. His eye fell on the swimmer/non-swimmer column. All parents were asked about this, as the school was by the river and non-swimmers were given priority lessons in the first few weeks. Chen See Lee could swim, but Han Pwee Lah could not. Problem solved, thought Brandon smugly.

'Can you swim?' he asked. He pointed at the girl and made a breaststroke movement with his arms.

It certainly wiped the smile off the girl's face. She cocked her head to one side and stared at him. Brandon was not daunted. He changed his stroke to front crawl, cutting his outstretched arms through imaginary water and moving his head from side to side, breathing out in short spurts.

The girl took a step backwards, and looked nervously behind her at the train, which was about to pull out.

'Oh for pity's sake,' Brandon said, his patience easily exhausted, as usual. 'Yes, you might well look worried. Get back on the train, young woman. Take a slow boat back to China, and do us all a favour.'

'Right, let's have a go,' said a voice. Brandon turned to see one of the new girls, with a mass of untidy dark curls and a very businesslike expression. She waved to the Chinese girl, and pointed to herself. 'Annie,' she said. 'Hi.'

The girl waved back, pointed at herself and said something no one could understand.

Annie fished in her own blazer pocket for an envelope which bore on it her name and address. Inside were the details the school had sent her of the arrangements for the first day of term. She offered it to the girl, who took it and looked at the name on the outside. Then the girl took out from her own pocket a similar envelope and gave it to Annie.

With a triumphant smile, Annie handed the envelope over to Brandon. 'Her name is Sonja Tapone. She's from Finland.'

'Finnish!' Brandon checked his list. 'Yep. There she is. Can't swim, either. Finnish! Well I never . . . well done. Smart thinking – good girl.'

Annie smiled mischievously. 'At my own poor humble comprehensive school in Bradford,' she said pointedly, 'before my dad won the lottery and decided I needed to learn to talk proper and polish up my manners, we were taught not to assume things. We were taught not to make judgements just by looking at people. But that was in Bradford. I guess we didn't know any better, eh?'

She smiled and took Sonja by the arm. 'I'll take her to the coach, shall I? And you can tick me off, an' all. Annie Tompkin.

Right, come on, kiddo.' She led Sonja off to the coach.

'That's what I call Attitude with a capital "A",' said Brandon.

'I like her already,' Stephanie laughed, and patted his arm. 'There, there, Brandon. It's about time someone took you on. She's absolutely right – you made assumptions, and you shouldn't have.'

Brandon grunted, and went back to ticking off names. Finally, everyone was on the coach, and Stephanie indicated to Manfred that it was time to leave.

Annie and Sonja were already striking up something of a conversation, with the aid of much sign language and a small drawing pad.

'May I join in?'

Annie looked up from the pad to see a tall, graceful-looking girl of about her own age looking at her with a shy smile.

'Sure. I'm Annie, and this is Sonja.'

'Yes, I know. I was watching you with the teacher. I am Carin Kemp.'

Carin said something in an impenetrable language to Sonja, who immediately became quite excited and started to pour forth a torrent of strange words and elaborate hand movements. She appeared to be copying the teacher's attempts to swim on the station platform.

'Are you Finnish too?' asked Annie.

'No, British. But we lived in Sweden until I was ten. My mum's Swedish – Dad was the ambassador there. Finns and Swedes understand each other very well. Many Finns speak Swedish, actually.'

'What is Sonja saying?' asked Annie.

Carin laughed. 'She is very cross with the strange man who accosted her on the platform. He didn't introduce himself, and she's been told not to talk to strangers. Then when she didn't a very expensive three-piece suit, and a beautiful hippy-looking woman in a sea of blue and purple fabric, holding his hand.

Annie peered at them through the bus window. 'What a weird couple,' she said. 'Who on earth are they?'

Carin leaned over her shoulder. 'Well, that woman in blue is Petal Butterkiss, the famous film star. I'd know her anywhere. You must have seen some of her movies – they show them on Saturday afternoons nowadays, on the television. In her day, she was really famous. My dad still has posters of her in his study. And that man with her must be the head, Mr Asquith. She gave up her film career to marry him – hard to see why, isn't it? He looks so . . . ordinary.'

'Perhaps it is his very ordinariness which she finds attractive,' said Sonja. 'I think he looks kind and good. His suit is the only thing about him I do not like. It is too well tailored. A schoolmaster should have baggy trousers and a worn patch on his elbows. Otherwise, how can he show it is teaching about which he cares the most?'

As they got off the bus, the new pupils were grouped together to meet the headmaster. He moved towards them with a broad and genuine smile. 'Welcome, welcome to King Arthur's English Academy,' he said. 'I am looking forward to greeting you all personally in just a little while. But I know many of you have had a long journey and will be glad of refreshments. Tea is laid out in the dining-room – Miss Harvey here will show you the way. At five o'clock I will see you all again and give you the low-down on everything King Arthur's has to offer.'

Petal regarded the group with great interest. She was beautiful, with violet eyes and perfect skin. 'I guess you must represent every continent on the globe between you,' she said in a husky voice, her wide smile revealing brilliant white, straight teeth. Annie could see why Carin's dad liked to look at her picture. 'Here at King Arthur's Academy, we think of ourselves as a global family, linked in heart and soul through the great cosmic forces that shape our destiny. I hope you will all feel free to commune, soul by soul, with those cosmic forces and with each other. . .'

'Er, yes, my dear. But tea first, eh?' interrupted Charles with a nervous smile. Once Petal had launched into the cosmic forces it would be difficult to retrieve her from them. 'Stephanie, could you lead the way to the dining-room? Thank you so much.'

The newcomers all trooped off after Stephanie. Brandon buttonholed Sonja as she followed the line. He mimed eating with a knife and fork, making loud chewing noises. Then he pointed at the door where the rest of the party were headed. 'Food,' he said with very obvious pity for the dumb idiot who had no idea what was going on. 'And drink. In there.' He mimed taking a drink, rubbed his stomach and pointed at the door again.

Sonja stood stock-still, staring at him with wide, astonished eyes. Annie waited for her to say something, but she simply shrugged her shoulders and looked questioningly at the teacher. He repeated the mime, with even more elaborate gestures and noises than before. Annie and Carin could not stop themselves laughing. Still Sonja did not let on that she could understand the teacher, who became steadily more red in the face as he tried to communicate with her.

'You must be thick as well as foreign,' said Brandon finally under his breath, just loud enough for Sonja to hear but not anyone else.

'It's all right, sir,' said Carin politely. 'We'll take her.' She turned to Sonja. 'Come with me,' she said in a very slow, clear voice. 'Me Car-in. Friend.'

Sonja smiled and took her arm.

The three were a little behind the rest of the crowd now, and as they moved towards the dining-room they heard Charles Asquith gently explaining to his wife that the cosmic forces were not something he felt should be discussed quite this early in the term. 'Let them settle in first, my dove,' he said. 'There will be plenty of time for those who share your interest to seek you out, once they've got to grips with school life.'

'You always say that, Charles,' said Petal plaintively. 'But last year the astrology circle and the food karma group between them numbered fewer than a dozen . . .' The pair disappeared through another door.

'Well,' said Annie. 'That's not what I pictured when they told me I were coming to a posh school. That headmaster looks a nice enough bloke – did you see his eyes twinkle when he smiled? Back at my old school, the head only smiled like that when he was being really, really nasty – although he smiled at my dad quite a lot after the papers said how much money we'd won in the lottery.'

'Was it a lot?' asked Sonja.

'Buckets of the stuff,' smiled Annie. 'So there we were: new house, new car, me dad set up in his own business, the works. Then he got this bee in his bonnet about me having all the chances he'd never had. And me mam started going on about how she'd love me to go to boarding-school and learn how to do all the things they do at posh parties and stuff. Me, I was quite happy where I was. Bradford High had its faults, but it was OK, and I managed to have a good time in spite of the teachers doing their best to make us work like slaves. It was fine for my mum and dad, too, until they got the money. Then suddenly it wasn't a good school any more . . .'

Annie's voice tailed off. She did not want to be disloyal to her parents, and she did understand that they only wanted what they thought was the best for her. She had tried not to show it, but Annie was actually quite angry at the way Mum and Dad had just decided to change her life and expected her to be as enthusiastic as they were.

'Well,' she said, 'let's just put it this way. They chose this school for one reason alone: it was the most expensive. Do you know it costs more to come here than Eton? They figured it had to be a good school, to charge that much.'

'Hmm. Possibly,' said Carin. 'Or possibly it takes people who don't know what an English school should cost. Most of us seem to be from another country, don't we? And how are our parents to know what goes on at Eton?'

'Why are you here then?' asked Annie.

Carin shrugged. 'Where my parents are working at the moment, there is no suitable school for nearly two hundred kilometres. I would have to go to boarding-school anyway – and my parents felt an English education would be the best in the world.'

'Mine too,' agreed Sonja.

Annie snorted. 'I feel very sorry for all the kids in other countries, if that's the case.'

'It is generally accepted,' said Sonja primly. 'It is certainly good for one's English to be taught in that language. It greatly improves grammar and fluency and so on.'

Annie laughed. 'You kill me,' she said. 'Your English is tons better than mine, and I'm the one who's gone through the English schools, not you. Ah well. You may be right. If we manage to survive the place – and in my case, I have to say I've got my doubts about that – it might have been worth all the upheaval. We may all come out elegant, cultured geniuses after all. Anyway, if I come out of this school with an upper-crust accent and using the right knife and fork at a posh party, both my parents will think it's money well spent.'

'But didn't you mind leaving your old home and friends?' asked Carin.

'Yeah. I did. I do. But as Mum says, I haven't really left me friends behind. Things are just a bit different – mostly in a nice way. After I moved, Gayle and Emma came round all the time. None of us could really believe our luck – we had a swimming-pool, a huge room just to muck about in, all the latest CD and video stuff . . . we went on a bit of a spending spree at first. Now I'm away at school, we'll still write and get together at the holidays. It meant so much to Mum and Dad to see me go up in the world, as they put it. I couldn't say No.'

Actually, Annie remembered with a grimace, she had said 'No' quite a lot. They had finally worn her down, Mum especially. She had always dreamed of having enough money to give Annie a 'good start in life'. Annie's mum, when she was a child, had read all the comics and books that described the lifestyle of the rich and famous. Boarding-school was a part of all that.

'They wanted me to come here really badly,' Annie said finally. 'Anyway, I like things to keep on the move – life gets boring, else. So I said OK, I'd give it a go for one year. It's not even a whole year, once you take away the holiday breaks. It's only a few weeks at a time. I think I can manage that. I'll try, anyway. If I really don't like it, I'll just go back to where I was. At least I'll have given it a go – my parents wouldn't expect more than that.'

'I hope you stay,' said Carin. 'Because I have to, whether I like it or not.'

'It's not as bad as I expected, so far,' said Annie. 'And I've met you two already. But to be honest, it's a bit weird and wacky for my taste. Still, we'll see. Come on. I can smell something really good, and my tummy's just getting the message that there's grub in the offing.'

They entered the building and followed the flow of people into the dining-hall. Annie was amazed at the wood panelling all around the walls, and the long carved oak tables and proper dining chairs. On the tables were china plates, cloth napkins and drinking glasses which shone in the glow of chandeliers casting a warm light over a room which would otherwise have been quite dark even in daylight. Not for King Arthur's the Formica-topped rectangles of Bradford High, which folded in two when the dining-hall became the drama studio.

It looked like a posh hotel. Annie felt nervous. It wasn't the sort of place she felt very comfortable in as an everyday thing. Did the other pupils feel at home here? Was Annie going to be completely different, like those kids she used to feel sorry for at Bradford High? They were the kind who just didn't have a clue what was going on. They stood out like sore thumbs, and no one wanted to be friends with them.

Don't be daft, she said to herself sternly. You've already met two people who look like they could be friends. It's not the end of the world. You'll be fine.

All the same, her stomach was tying a knot in itself as she moved to sit down. She was so absorbed in trying to look like she was a part of this strange scene, and still looking around at all the details of the beautiful room, that she was not paying any attention to the person already seated as Annie slid into the neighbouring chair. She had only a blurred image out of the corner of her eye of a hairy-looking small boy. Very small, actually. And very hairy.

Annie looked properly, and gasped. She jumped out of her

seat. Sonja and Carin, who had been deep in conversation in Swedish, were staring at their table companion with their mouths open and their eyes wide, like matching souvenir book-ends.

It was a chimpanzee, in full King Arthur's English Academy uniform. He was calmly munching his way through a plate of scones, taking a bite and then stretching his chimpanzee arm over the table to take food from other plates. His napkin was tucked into his blazer, and he sat on his chair like a wizened little old man.

'What the . . . ?' Annie didn't know what to say. Wildly, she looked around the room. No one seemed too bothered by the chimp – a few of the new pupils were looking over and laughing, but generally it seemed as though meeting a chimp at the tea table was no big deal.

'His name's Lynchpin,' said an older, brown-haired girl with glasses. She was sitting on the other side of the chimp, and as she spoke his name he put his arm round her and climbed on to her lap, snuggling down like a toddler. 'I'm Lindy Wappleback, by the way. Hi. You're new, aren't you? Welcome to King Arthur's.'

'Er, hi. I'm Annie. But what is, um, Lynchpin . . . ? Why . . . I mean . . . well . . . what's he here for?'

The girl smiled. 'He's my companion. I've reared him since he was tiny. My dad has a colony of them – he researches primates.'

'He's not that one who does the telly programmes on BBC 2?' asked Annie.

'Sure, that's him. "The Power of the Primates". Horace Wappleback is my dad. Lynchpin is the son of Maisie, star of the show. Anyhow, we've always been together. Dad travels back to the States a lot these days, and Mum runs the colony.

But Lynchpin gets real sick when I'm away at school. So we enrolled him.'

'You enrolled a chimp? You mean, you pay fees for him, and that?'

Lindy shrugged. 'Sure. The headmaster took a bit of persuading, but Lynchpin pays his bills on time and is a very undemanding student. You'd be surprised how much chimps can do. I bet he's streets ahead of some of the students here. He's not going to pass any exams, but what the heck? Neither am I. My parents don't believe in exams. We should just, you know, let it all flow. And at King Arthur's, as long as you pay the fees and don't make misery for anyone else, that's pretty much what happens. Lynchpin and I just fit right in.'

Sonja and Carin had recovered slightly from the shock by now, and were regarding the chimp with a mixture of disapproval and fascination.

'Excuse me,' said Sonja darkly. 'We have not been introduced, and I do not wish to be offensive, but I do not think it is seemly or hygienic to eat at table with animals. Please do not allow your . . . companion to maul my scone and jam the way he makes free with your own.'

Lynchpin was crumbling Lindy's scone and spreading jam all over her plate.

'No offence,' said Lindy easily. 'I know he's a bit too much to take in at first. But you'll get used to him. He only eats tea with me – the rest of the time he eats in our room. But he does come to lessons, so you'll see him in the gym and stuff like that. Don't worry, he's just like you most of the time. He only reverts to chimp now and then. Say, are you Chinese? You have a real weird accent.'

'I am from a very remote part of China,' said Sonja without hesitation. 'Shan Chong Province. I expect you've heard of it?'

'I . . .' Lindy did not want to appear rude. 'Oh, sure . . . I think so . . .'

'You probably remember it because of the documentary on the television last year, and because of our local delicacy, which would be particularly memorable in your case.'

'I . . .' Lindy shook her head. 'No, I don't remember. What is the local delicacy?'

Sonja did not answer. She looked meaningfully at Lynchpin.

'Oh my gosh. You don't mean . . . how could you?' Lindy gathered up her chimpanzee and rose to her feet, clutching him against her chest.

Sonja shrugged. 'Don't worry. I only revert to native behaviour now and then.'

Lindy and Lynchpin fled the room, and Sonja reached for a scone.

'Why did you say that?' asked Carin.

'Why not?' said Sonja.

Carin and Annie looked at each other. Carin raised her eyebrows, and Annie shrugged. They both stared at Sonja.

'You're amazing,' said Annie. 'I hope we're going to be friends, because I surely wouldn't want to cross you.'

'Just don't call me Chinese. No offence to China, but I am Finnish. I am proud to be Finnish. It is offensive to make judgements about people because of the way they look. Besides, I do not want to eat with a chimpanzee. I do not think Lynchpin will be seated near me in future, do you?'

Annie smiled, but inside the knot tied itself a bit tighter. She was more sure than ever that she was never going to fit in. Even the girl she hoped to have as a friend was shaping up to be seriously weird. And what kind of school enrolled an ape?

Chapter 2

*I*n the headmaster's sitting-room, Charles Edward Asquith, headmaster of the King Arthur's English Academy, took the cup and saucer his wife offered him and strode to the window. He loved the first day of autumn term. The neatly clipped school lawns and the gravel drive which swept up to the main entrance were immaculate. Across the quadrangle the leaded windows of Old School House blinked in the sunlight. Behind the old buildings, down towards the river, he could just see the domed roof of the new Pecking Betty Science Block (sponsored by Pecking Betty Records) shining like silver where it caught the light. In the distance the road snaked over the hills towards the station, where the school bus faithfully toiled away, bringing yet another load of King Arthur's' fresh and hopeful young students to begin the new school year.

'Delightful,' he sighed.

He raised the delicate china cup to his lips and sipped at the tea his wife had prepared for him.

'Aagh!' Charles spat the disgusting liquid out at once, all his senses telling him it had to be something deeply poisonous. The cup slipped; his expensive Italian suit was badly splashed. Suspiciously, Charles examined the contents which remained in the cup. He had taken it automatically, but now he looked closely he could see it did not look like his usual afternoon tea at all. It was dark green, for a start, and had tiny bits floating in it.

'What on earth . . . ?' Charles turned to his wife, who sat at the table, reading the *New York Times* and eating a pile of banana and mango slices with a silver fork.

'Petal, my dear – what is this in my cup? It's rather . . . well, frankly, Petal, it's about as appetising as horses' urine.'

Petal looked up from her paper with a pleasant smile. 'When on earth did you drink horses' urine?'

Charles ignored this remark. 'What is it, Petal?'

'It's a new recipe,' said Petal calmly. 'It purges you of all the evil toxins which flood your body.' Her expression darkened, and she gave him one of her tragic heroine looks. 'We invite peril and destruction if we interfere with that very fine balance of body and soul, you know.'

Charles sighed. She had been at one of her group meetings again. Charles loved his wife dearly – and there was no doubt that she was good for business, being so famous. But even Charles could see that she was as batty as a coot.

The village of Morton Gipping, just down the road, attracted batty people because it was rumoured that King Arthur had passed through on the way to his burial ground near by. Lot of nonsense, of course, but batty people go for nonsense in a big way, don't they? So they had the Morton Gipping King Arthur Society, the New Age, New World for Morton Gipping Campaign, the Queen Guinevere's Hug-a-Tree Society, the Lancelot Yoga, Health and Fitness Club, and the King Arthur Karma Fellowship. His wife belonged to them all. What's more, they'd all given her free membership and countless invitations to social events held by all the other batty coots in the area, because she was Petal Butterkiss, the famous American actress of stage and screen. She had become even more famous when she gave it all up for the love of a charming English schoolmaster. Overnight, she went from the face in every showbiz magazine as the leading dizzy-blonde-in-need-of-a-big-strong-hero-to-protect-her-from-danger, to the face in every women's magazine as the woman-prepared-to-make-the-ultimate-sacrifice-of-a-glittering-career. She was, she said, quite content to retire to the English countryside.

But fame followed Petal, and her fortune came in handy too. Within three years of their wedding, Charles and Petal Asquith took over the crumbling buildings, moved in an army of builders and renovators, and the King Arthur's English Academy was born.

These days the school was known internationally as the place where 'new money', such as rock stars and lottery winners, sent their children to be educated in the finer points of a proper English upbringing. If you wanted your children to hobnob with the rich and famous, it was the top place to be. The facilities were superb, and some of the children even passed their exams. But Charles had discovered a sizeable number of very wealthy people who didn't actually care too much about good exam results. These were not children who would have to compete for jobs, after all. What their parents wanted from them was charm, discretion, good looks and all the social graces which would label them as Somebodys anywhere in the world. It was what Charles's marketing lecturer on the business studies course had called 'a gap in the market'. Charles had identified this gap and plugged it.

At King Arthur's Academy, looks, charm and tradition were far more important than mere academic success. Bright scholars were not actively discouraged, but since the teachers were picked primarily for their looks and their ability to fit the image of the school, rather than their ability to teach, life was easier if you didn't have a genuine thirst for knowledge. The visual impact of the school and its staff to visiting parents, who were mostly from the glossy, image-conscious worlds of entertainment and politics, was very important. Some of the teachers were good at teaching, but this was pure luck.

'I'm sorry, Petal, I just can't drink this.' Charles placed the cup and saucer down at his wife's side and kissed her cheek.

'We must all find our own path,' she muttered darkly, and returned to the *New York Times*.

'And please, Petal, don't offer it to the new parents. Promise me you'll serve up proper tea – the Assam, or perhaps the Earl Grey.'

Petal swept her eyelashes in his direction and gave him the full benefit of those huge, dark violet eyes. They had turned thousands of men's knees to water, and they made it difficult to deny Petal anything.

'Bunny Beaver, that would be like pouring toxic waste in a cup. I agree this is a teensy weensy bit bitter . . . I expect it's the ivy root that did it. If I added a little honey . . .'

'No,' said Charles firmly. 'Absolutely not. Regular tea, Petal. None of the funny stuff. Do you promise?'

Petal looked disappointed. 'If you insist,' she said.

'Thank you. Now, I must be going. Mr and Mrs Pankinella are being given a tour of the school, but they'll arrive at my study any minute, and I have to change my suit.' Charles straightened his stained waistcoat and looked meaningfully at his wife. She smiled sweetly and poured herself some more of the foul brew she had given to him.

'Very well, Bunny. I'll have a regular teapot full of the ghastly death brew you call tea ready for them. And there'll be oat and raisin cookies today.'

'Have you been baking, my love?' asked Charles with some anxiety.

'No, Pumpkin. I gave Mrs Barton the recipe.'

Charles gave a deep sigh of relief. Mrs Barton had been the school cook long enough to become very experienced in adapting Petal's recipes into something you could actually eat. 'That's very thoughtful of you, Petal. See you soon, then.'

Petal was always invited to take tea with visitors to the school but sometimes Charles tried very hard to discourage her. He called it 'stopping her from overworking herself'. She was touched by his concern, although she had noted that this concern was usually expressed most keenly when the visitors were rather dull, ordinary people. Charles worried that she was too exotic for the traditional English image he tried so hard to create. He thought actors and musicians would be all right with Petal, but not politicians or bankers. If only Petal could reassure him. She loved the role of English headmaster's wife. She really believed that she was perfect for the part. Charles worried too much.

If only he would let her have a free hand with what the dear children were eating. Petal could offer them her unique Yin Yang scones, or even the karma cookies, instead of those ghastly supermarket things with the shiny wrappers. The King Arthur Karma Fellowship had now perfected its wholesome cookie recipe after hours in kitchens around the village, looking for just the right vibes in the right atmosphere. Mrs Florence Yobbit, of Gawain Cottage, had finally cracked the problem; she achieved, in her extensive kitchen experiments, the perfect balance of herbs and weed extract for aiding the soul's journey through life. It was generally agreed that once this formula had been incorporated into everyone's basic diet, the true balance of nature and the human body would be achieved across the globe. Charles, however, would not listen to her pleas to instruct the school in the Karmic Eating Plan for a Healthy Body and a Healthy Soul. He said the children would prefer chips.

Mr and Mrs Pankinella, a rock musician and a backing singer, arrived at Charles's study half an hour late. They didn't offer any explanation, just smiled gravely and shook his hand. Their son, Lance, was a sullen, uncommunicative teenager who grunted from behind a curious curtain of sleek, dark hair which had been carefully cut to completely obscure his eyes. His parents, however, looked more like a couple of merchant bankers than rock musicians. They wore sober suits in grey and damson wool respectively, and Mr Pankinella had even shaved the day before. They explained that their band, Rocking Fist, was on a lengthy tour of Europe. After that they would be 'cutting a couple of albums' at a studio in London before returning to the States. Lance was to be a pupil at King Arthur's at least for the next two years.

'We want to give him a sense of stability,' said his mother primly, 'and enable him to develop normally and to his full potential.' She sounded like a headmistress.

'Well, Lance, are you a musician too?' asked Charles.

'Nah,' said Lance.

'But you must be a big fan of your parents, eh? Such talent . . . I expect you're very proud.'

Lance shrugged.

'So tell me, what are your interests?' asked Charles, determined to make conversation.

'None,' said Lance.

'None?' Charles tried to smile encouragingly. 'Come now, there must be something that excites you. What do you like to do in your spare time?'

'Nothin',' said Lance.

'Nothing at all?'

Lance shrugged. 'TV,' he said finally.

'Then I hope your tour of the school included the wonderful Lilac Lil Leisure Complex, just by the science block,' said Charles. 'We have five lounges, with a television in each, so there won't be any squabbles about what channel to watch.'

For the first time, Lance looked up and peered through his hair with a faint sign of interest. 'Cable?' he asked.

'Ah. Unfortunately not. Actually, most of our students find themselves very busy with the wide variety of more traditional activities on offer here. Television isn't such a popular attraction as you might expect . . .'

'Jees,' said Lance, and disappeared behind his hair again.

Charles's smile was beginning to ache. 'Right,' he said, trying not to grit his teeth. 'I'll just get my secretary to take you along to the dining-hall, Lance. Some of the students are already tucking into a lovely tea, and we don't want you to miss out, do we? Meanwhile, I'll take your parents off to have a chat with me and fill out the forms and so on and you can all meet up later to say goodbye. Is that all right?'

'Sure,' said Lance. He left the room without a backward glance or a word to his parents. Miss George was waiting outside to escort him to the dining-room.

'Off you go then, Lance,' said Charles. 'Perhaps you'll make some new friends over tea, eh? That's the spirit.'

He watched the lad slope off behind Miss George with a sinking heart. New friends? Unlikely. And if he wasn't happy at school, his parents were unlikely to be showing their gratitude by contributing to the new swimming-pool complex. Ah well . . .

Poor Petal, thought Charles as he turned back to the rather sour-looking pair who had brought Lance into the world. She had been so excited at the prospect of Rocking Fist being associated with the school. She had hoped Lance would start a rock band, and invite Petal to be their manager. Charles had never heard of Rocking Fist, but Petal had squealed with excitement when he read her the application letter. For two days she sang Rocking Fist hits lustily as she went about her daily chores, and Charles began to understand why he had never become a fan:

> *Ooh, ah, you know I love you, baby,*
> *Baby yeh, baby dooh, baby yeh, yeh, yeh.*
> *I'll always love you, baby, I will, baby,*
> *'Cos you're not going nowhere,*
> *Except to my heart, it's true, baby, yeh.*

Petal would be disappointed to meet Mr Pankinella in the flesh. She had pointed him out to Charles on 'Top of the Pops' – all black leather and wild hair, which in Mr Pankinella's case had looked dangerously entangled with a large round earring in his left ear. Petal had thought it very stylish. Today, Mr Pankinella had his hair scraped back severely from his face into a ponytail, and no jewellery in sight. Charles had discovered over the years that it was often the way with people who made their living by outraging decent, honourable folk. They turned out to be ten times more decent and honourable than the people they outraged. Ah well. Never mind. They were very rich and very famous, and perhaps in time Lance could be coaxed into stringing a few words together and even coming up with a sentence or two. Charles would see it as his personal challenge to get to know the lad and improve his communication skills.

In the dining-room Annie, Sonja and Carin were chatting away between mouthfuls of cake. There seemed to be a never-ending supply, as uniformed waiters kept the cake plates stacked.

'Well, so far I think it has the edge over Bradford High,' said Annie. 'Ooh, if Gayle and Emma could see me now, they'd be sick as parrots. I bet they're sharing a KitKat in a corner of the park by the bins at this very moment.' Annie remembered, with a surge of homesickness, how they had divided that fourth finger of chocolate into pieces; they had become quite expert at getting equal shares. Now Gail and Emma would not have that problem. She wondered if they thought of her, as they shared their chocolate every day. She wished she could see them.

The places left vacant by Lindy and Lynchpin had been discreetly cleaned up by one of the waiters, and Annie emerged from a very tasty scone with cream and jam to find the seat opposite her had been taken by a boy of about her own age with long dark hair which completely covered his eyes. He was not eating, just sipping some orange juice and studying the grain of the table, as far as she could see.

'Hiya,' said Annie with a friendly grin. 'Are you new here, an' all?'

'Yep,' the boy said. He might have been looking at her, or still at the table: it was difficult to tell.

'I'm Annie. This is Sonja, and this is Carin,' Annie pointed at her friends in turn. 'Sonja's from Finland, Carin's from Sweden, and I'm from Bradford.'

'Uh-huh,' grunted the boy.

'So, are you gonna tell us who you are, then?'

'Lance,' said the boy.

'Where are you from, Lance?' asked Carin politely.

'US of A,' said Lance.

'What do you think of the place so far?' asked Annie.

Lance shrugged. 'OK.'

'Are you always so talkative, Lance?' asked Annie.

'Nope,' said Lance. He took a scone, and began to eat it. Annie caught a flash of very blue eyes as he parted his hair to get at the scone, and a swift smile. She smiled back.

'I don't know if you've copped the head and his wife,' said Annie, 'but they look a very odd pair. And we've already found at least one real eejit on the staff . . .' Annie, who was born to chat, launched into her account of their first meeting with Brandon on the station and how Sonja had pretended not to know any English. Lance's hair waved slightly as he turned his head, presumably to look at Sonja. 'Cool,' he said.

Annie found Lance very intriguing. She was used to people who chatted, maybe not saying anything very much but saying a lot of it, to let you know they were interested in being friends. She couldn't make out what was going on with Lance. 'Do you know anyone here?' she asked him.

'Nope,' said Lance.

'Well, you can go around with us if you like,' said Annie. 'Now that we've chatted, I feel I know all about you.' She laughed, and was rewarded with another flash of blue eye.

'Sure,' said Lance.

A disturbance at the other end of the table caught their attention. A tall African boy in a gold brocaded costume complete with hat, had sprung to his feet. 'Where are the servants?' he demanded indignantly. 'I have waited for several minutes for someone to apply to this cake the butter for me . . .' He held out a scone. 'It is an insult to my people to so offend their prince!'

There was a lot of laughing at this, followed by an awkward silence when those around him realised the boy was not joking – he was genuinely outraged. One of the students at his table informed him, none too graciously, that if he didn't butter the scone himself, it certainly wasn't going to be done for him.

'This is not supportable!' exclaimed the boy, and he stormed off into the kitchen at the far end of the dining-hall, carrying his scone in his hand.

'What on earth is all that about?' asked Annie. 'Who does he think he is?'

'He's obviously someone very important,' said Carin. 'When we lived in Nairobi, Dad had a regular circuit round some smaller African states, and we sometimes went with him. The top families have servants to do everything. They don't even dress themselves. The poor lad must have thought it was the same in England.'

'You mean he doesn't even expect to dress or to feed himself?' asked Sonja. She looked very disapproving. 'It is not seemly to be waited on hand and foot. In Finland, we don't have such people who expect others to do everything for them.'

'I wouldn't mind it, meself,' said Annie. 'For a while, anyway. So, will he starve, I wonder? Or will someone take pity on him and teach him how to use a knife?'

The boy returned to the table a couple of minutes later. Before sitting down, he bowed to the people sitting round his end of the table. 'I do so humbly apology,' he said in a booming voice which could be heard in every corner of the hall. 'I have misunderstood the customs of your land. Forgive me if I seemed perfensive. I will have my own staff sent over from my diminion. Until then, I will not trouble upon you to wait for me.' He sat down at the table and cut open his scone. His neighbour passed the butter, and all was quiet again.

'Cool,' said Lance.

'Fruitcake,' said Annie.

At five o'clock promptly the headmaster appeared, wearing

a different but equally expensive suit. His exotic wife was nowhere to be seen, but he was accompanied by a man in a grey suit (Marks and Spencer's, thought Annie, not from the head's tailor) and a woman in a nurse's uniform.

'Let me welcome you once more to King Arthur's English Academy,' said Charles Asquith. 'And I would like to introduce you to two of our staff with whom I am sure you will have dealings. First, Mr Clingon, our bursar. Mr Clingon runs the finances of the school, and an admirable job he does too. Mr Clingon's name will already be known to your parents, as it is he who sends out the dreaded fee bills at the start of each term.'

Mr Clingon gave everyone a furtive smile.

'But he is also available to give financial advice to any of you whose investment portfolios are in need of expert consideration, or to those whose parents wish to set up income plans for them during their time at the school. For a small fee, Mr Clingon is only too delighted to ensure that your allowance is looked after properly, not frittered away on fripperies at the start of the term. And finally, should any of your parents be thinking in terms of endowments to the school, or memorial gifts or facilities, Mr Clingon is available to advise on the most suitable presentation.'

'Me dad would love this,' said Annie. 'Talk about starting as you mean to go on. Dad said the headmaster sounded like a right smoothie on the phone – he's right, an' all. I wouldn't buy a used car from that Clingon though – he looks a bit shifty to me.'

'Shark,' said Lance.

'Yeah, shark,' said Annie.

The nurse was explaining to the pupils that she was available at any time for an emergency, but that she would prefer it if they could please have their aches and pains or chickenpox or whatever during the school day, as this would be easier to manage. There followed a very complicated explanation of how to get to the sick bay, or rather the 'twelve-bedded Cutlass Insurance Services Sanatorium which is fully equipped to deal with most things, short of broken bones and major burns – oh, and earthquakes of course.'

'I didn't know England had earthquakes,' said Sonja nervously.

'I think that's supposed to be a joke,' said Annie.

The journey to the sanatorium seemed to involve quite a long hike round the back of the main building and across the river. Annie decided it would be easier just not to get sick. You'd be half dead by the time you found the place.

Nurse Guptah launched into a list of all the common illnesses they might experience, and the main symptoms. She assured them that if they had any of these symptoms – 'any at all,' she said emphatically – they were to come and see her 'at once. And even if you're not sick, but just need someone to talk to,' she continued in a low voice, 'homesick, lonely, trouble with bullies or even just very spotty . . .'

'I think we get the picture, Nurse Guptah. Thank you very much,' said Charles.

Nurse Guptah looked a bit crestfallen. She had been about to explain what help she could offer with acne, and how it wasn't such a good idea to just stick a pin in your spots and hope for the best. But Mr Asquith smiled at her and murmured, 'Splendid, Amina – just the right tone,' and she cheered up.

'Now I'm sure you would all like to see your rooms and get settled in,' said Charles to the pupils. 'Those of you who are returners will of course be in the same rooms as last year and can find your own way there when you're ready. Our new students will be shown to their rooms in about fifteen minutes. We'll come and give you a call. Enjoy your tea, enjoy meeting each other, and make use of all the leisure and sports facilities this evening to get relaxed and fit for tomorrow. We start at two o'clock sharp tomorrow afternoon, with assembly in the main hall which you saw as you came into the building. Goodbye until then.'

The head and his little entourage left, and the noise of excited chatter resumed once more.

Annie tried to imagine what it would be like going to bed without seeing her parents sitting in the living-room, and kissing them goodnight. For the first time she felt a wave of longing to be back at home, mucking about with Gayle and copying someone else's homework ready for the daily grind at Bradford High. Too late now, she thought. I said I'd give it a go, and I'll not back out. Whatever happens, I've got to stick it out for a year like I promised. Then I can go back to Bradford High and Mum and Dad will never bother me again about trying to better meself, whatever that means.

A year had not seemed such a long time when Annie agreed to her parents' plan. Now it stretched ahead like a yawning chasm which she could not imagine getting past. As they were collected from their tables in groups, Annie lagged behind Sonja, Carin and Lance a little. She reached into her pocket and touched the photograph of her mum and dad sitting in the garden at home. It was not spectacular, life in Bradford. It was not unpredictable or exciting. But it was good, and it was familiar. Annie was beginning to feel that she had dropped on to another planet, a sort of fabulously wealthy and comfortable version of hell. The only reason she was laughing along with Carin and Sonja at the antics of the African boy and Lindy with her chimpanzee was because she didn't want to cry.

'Are you OK?' asked a boy beside her. He looked normal enough.

Annie smiled. 'Yeah. Just . . . well, a bit homesick. I've never been away before.'

'Lucky you,' said the boy. 'I've been at boarding-school since I was six years old. Believe me, this place is heaven compared to most of them.'

Six years old. Annie tried to picture herself at six, to imagine what it would have been like to leave Mum and Dad and go away to school. She couldn't imagine it. There was only a wave of blinding horror at the thought.

'How long have you been here?' she asked. 'I'm Annie, by the way.'

'I'm Franz. I've been here nearly three years. It takes some getting used to, but you'll settle in. We all do, in the end. See you around.'

Franz went to move away, but Annie grabbed his arm. 'You are normal, aren't you?' she asked suddenly. 'I know it's a really weird question and makes *me* look like the cooky one, but . . . do you have chimpanzees, or servants or anything?'

Franz laughed. 'You've met Lynchpin. Yes, I am normal. I think so, anyway. I did have to leave my last school because of an unfortunate accident in the science labs, but otherwise I had a blameless and very ordinary early childhood.'

'What did you do?' asked Annie.

'I burned the place down,' said Franz. 'But I promise you it was an accident. King Arthur's was the only school which would take me. The headmaster is a nice man. He believed me that it was an experiment that went wrong.'

'You . . . don't do experiments now, do you?' asked Annie nervously. Great, she thought. A hell-hole with a resident arsonist.

'Of course I do experiments,' said Franz with a grin. 'But only in the science lab. And only when the teacher is present. I am not allowed to work on my own in there.' He bowed slightly. 'I must go, Annie. It was a pleasure to meet you. I hope you manage to find some more normal people. There are plenty of us about, I promise.'

Annie could only hope he was telling the truth.

Chapter 3

*T*hey were shown to their rooms by Nurse Guptah. Unless people starting at the school had specially requested to share with someone, they were given rooms at random. When Annie asked if the girls could stay together in one of the four-bed rooms, Nurse Guptah readily agreed.

'How nice that you've made friends already,' she said with a smile. 'That's what we like to see. Mind you, if you're feeling at all homesick or lonely, you must come over to the sanatorium. I'm only too pleased . . .' she tailed off, as if expecting someone to interrupt. Annie got the impression that Nurse Guptah was rather lonely herself.

'Perhaps we can just come over to say hello sometime,' she said.

'Ooh yes!' Nurse Guptah almost shrieked with excitement. 'That would be . . .' She recovered herself and said more calmly, 'That would be all right, if you feel the need . . . Now, we need a fourth. Who would like to go in with these three?'

No one answered straight away, since everyone felt a bit self-conscious. But Carin spotted a small, dark, sporty-looking girl looking wistfully at them, and smiled at her. The girl put up her hand. 'Fine,' said Nurse Guptah. 'And you are . . . ?'

'Natalie de Suza,' said the girl. With a shy smile, she followed the three into the room, and Nurse Guptah led the others off down the hall.

Once inside, the girls looked around them with approval. The rooms were large and had enormous bay windows overlooking lawns at the back of the school. There was a small armchair, a locker, chest of drawers and wardrobe by each bed. Pushed against the wall were wicker screens which could be pulled round for privacy. Underneath the windows ran a window seat, and in the centre of the room were four desks and chairs, each with a little bookcase.

'It's nice, isn't it?' said Annie. 'I must say I'm not used to sharing, but I'm glad now I didn't choose a room of my own.'

'I hope you don't mind . . . I mean, me,' said Natalie quietly. The other three smiled at her. She was a gentle-looking creature with huge brown eyes and an amazing number of freckles when you saw her close up. Right now she was looking pale and nervous, but Carin slipped an arm through hers and squeezed it.

'I could tell you're our kind of person,' she said. 'I'm Carin. This is Annie and Sonja. Swedish, Brit and Finn respectively.'

'Natalie. I'm not really from anywhere. I mean, I'm Irish, but Dad sort of travels a lot. I was born in Ireland, but we've lived in eight or nine countries since then.'

'What about your mum?' asked Annie.

Natalie blushed and looked away. 'I haven't . . . we don't see her. Which beds shall we have?'

Clearly she didn't want to talk about herself. They fell to choosing beds and desks, and unpacking. Sonja laughed when she came across a large box of biscuits which her mother had hidden away in her case, and explained that Mrs Tapone was convinced that there would not be enough food, because she had heard that English boarding-schools starved their children as part of the education process.

'I don't know where she got that idea,' laughed Carin. 'I could not move for scones and cream.'

'Me too,' said Annie. 'Still, I'm sure the bikkies will come in useful.'

'Shall we go for a walk before it gets dark?' asked Carin. 'The grounds look great – I think there's a fountain behind those hedges, if I remember the brochure correctly.'

The others readily agreed, and they set off on a tour. The gardens at King Arthur's were lovely. As well as the formal lawns they could see from their window, there was an apple orchard, a series of walled gardens with statues and benches and ponds, and a small woodland, full of trees which Sonja thought were very old. Sonja turned out to be a bit of a gardening expert, and was delighted with the variety she found. While she was exclaiming enthusiastically over what Annie thought was a pretty ordinary bush, Annie's eye was caught by movement over in the corner of the garden. Lance, the strange non-talker from tea, was moving towards a bench with the lad who had demanded a servant to butter his scone. Annie was intrigued. Lance was actually talking – quite a lot, from what she could see. The scone boy, as Annie thought of him, was listening and nodding, saying a few words here and there, but Lance was positively lively.

Annie wandered over to their bench. 'Hello again,' she said.

Lance looked up, or at least it appeared that way – no eye was yet visible. 'Hi,' he smiled.

'Good evening, Miss . . .' said the scone boy. He jumped to his feet and stretched out his hand.

'Annie,' said Annie with an amused smile. She took his hand, wincing slightly as he gripped it with all the force of a vice.

'I am Uem Taddugorrono, Lord of all the Highlands, Heir to the Golden Throne,' said the boy, and he bowed over her hand.

'Er . . . hi, um, Oo-who?'

'Say "Oo-em",' he offered politely. 'It is easy. It is only the second name "Tad-a-gor-rono" which proves difficult. But it is not necessary to use all names if we are to be friends – and if we are not, then there is no point in learning my name at all. Is that not so?'

'That's certainly logical,' laughed Annie. 'Oo-em will do, that's for sure. Now, did you get your scone buttered, or what?'

Uem looked away. 'I am covered with shame and emberriment,' he said.

'Embarrassment,' supplied Lance.

'Quite so,' said Uem. 'I have many things to learn about England and the English. That is of course why I am here. I telephoned to my father and asked for servants to be sent over straight away. But my wise father has informed me that if I am to learn English ways I must live the English life, and butter my own cakes. Alas, there are so many things I must do for myself now . . .' he sighed.

Lance jerked a thumb at his companion. 'Loaded,' he said to Annie.

'Well, I did kind of work that one out,' smiled Annie.

Lance jerked again. 'Royal,' he said.

'What, you mean like, really royal, not just pretending?'

Uem bowed slightly and nodded.

'Great!' said Annie. 'It'll do me dad proud to hear I've been hobnobbing with royalty.'

'Ah yes, the Hobnob. I have heard of this,' said Uem with enthusiasm. 'It is a very famous biscuit. Do you have one about your person? I would greatly enjoy to partake of such a beast.'

'Eh? Um . . . not just at the moment. Look, what were you talking about before I came along? Whatever it was, Lance here seems to have got more enthusiastic than a pig at trough.'

'Longhorns,' said Lance. He flicked his hair out of his eyes.

'Longhorns?' queried Annie. 'What are they?'

'Beetles.'

'This is a joke, yeah?'

'Nope,' said Lance.

Annie looked at Uem quizzically.

'Indeed, he is speaking the tooth,' said Uem.

'Truth,' Lance and Annie corrected together.

'Just so,' said Uem, with a bow. 'Lance is an expert on wood-boring beetles, and he was interested to hear about some of the specimens that are native to my country. I must confice that I believe Lance knows more about such creatures than I do. He has written the articles for journals and magazines. But he is very endearing on the subject, I assume you.'

Annie looked at Lance, who smiled back at her perfectly innocently. 'Wood-boring insects? You mean, like woodworm and that?'

'Yep,' Lance nodded.

'How do you get to be an expert on a thing like that?'

'Books, mostly.'

'Mmm. But why?'

'Why not?'

'You're doing it again,' said Annie, faintly irritated.

'What?' said Lance.

'What happened to all the strung-together sentences I saw you using a minute ago?'

Lance shrugged. 'Gone.'

'Gone? Just like that, eh? It's a limited supply, is it? One two-minute burst of conversation per day just about as much as you can manage?'

'Yep,' said Lance. He smiled teasingly at her, and his hair slipped over his face again.

'So, if I had not come from boring old Bradford, if you'll excuse the pun, which only has common-or-garden woodworm – if I'd come from the sort of place where more exotic wood munchers have a whale of a time destroying everything wooden they can get their little insect teeth into, then you'd talk to me like you did to Uem before we came along?'

'Sure,' said Lance.

Annie felt like hitting him and laughing at the same time. He was infuriating. He was looking at her now through his hair, she was sure.

'Actually . . .' said Lance.

'Actually what?' returned Annie.

'You're wrong on both counts, actually. First, Bradford does not only have woodworm in its range of wood-boring insect life. There have been some quite unusual specimens there which they say came over with imported timber, but which managed to survive the longest time in a climate which not even a Bradford person would say was mild, I imagine. So Bradford is not boring in wood-boring insect terms at all. And the other thing is that woodworm don't have teeth. It's maggots that actually eat the wood away. They hatch and bore their way through the wood until they become flies, and then they simply fly away. They're very small, so you don't see them. With some species of wood-borers, they leave the outside of a structure completely intact. From the outside you can't see them at all. But they're there, all right, in the beams of the roof perhaps, feeding away and destroying the wood from the inside out. By the time you know you've got a problem, the roof has caved in.'

'What lovely little creatures,' murmured Annie. 'Well, that's something to look forward to, isn't it?'

'Oh, you don't need to worry about it round here – or in Bradford. That particular beetle can only survive in very particular climates. In Great Britain, only Hampshire has just the right conditions.'

Annie stared at this strange boy, wondering if he was taking the mickey. He drew back his hair, and smiled at her, looking quite normal. 'Is that enough conversation for you? Or would you like to hear about the mating habits of longhorns, perhaps?'

'No. I have a feeling I don't. All right, you've proved you can talk. But is wood-boring insects the sole topic of conversation for you?'

Lance shrugged. 'Pretty much.' Down went the hair again. Annie was to learn that Lance lived by a simple philosophy: if you don't have anything to say, don't say anything. Wood-boring insects were his great passion in life: he could not say why, only that they were the most fascinating creatures on earth for him. But on most other topics he had little to say, and so conserved his energy.

Annie was also to learn that he was a good friend, and a laugh to be with. But all that was to be learned in the future. On that day in the garden, she only saw him as one more fruitcake in a school full of fruitcakes. He did not seem to be able to chatter, or indeed to want to.

Carin, Sonja and Natalie, who had been smelling all the plants and comparing fragrances, caught up with them and the whole introduction scene with Uem was played over again: they couldn't say his name either. Once that was over, Uem chatted very entertainingly, getting at least one word in every sentence wrong so that you had to listen hard to keep up. Lance nodded his head now and then, but was otherwise unnervingly silent. Uem explained that he and Lance had each opted for a room of their own, but they were next door to each other and had become acquainted. They had come into the garden to see if they could find the croquet lawn. Uem was anxious to play croquet, 'The most English of games,' as he called it.

'We were doing a tour of the grounds,' said Carin. 'We had almost finished, but we thought we would go back to the summerhouse down by the river, and follow the path through the woodland back to the house. We haven't found the croquet lawn yet, so it must be ahead of us. Want to come?'

'Sure,' said Lance.

'I would be eminently delighted to expect,' said Uem.

Carin raised her eyebrows, but said nothing.

They set off, with Annie and Uem doing most of the talking. As they rounded the bend in the path by the summerhouse, which had been hidden from view by high yew hedges, they saw that the summerhouse was occupied. There were two people sitting there, deep in conversation. One of them had a sheaf of papers which he was looking through. Neither man noticed the pupils until they were pretty close; close enough for Annie's sharp eyes to spot that the pages had a lot of columns of figures on them, a bit like Dad's accounts that she had helped him with before he won the lottery and could afford his own secretary.

'Good evening!' boomed Uem cheerfully. 'What a pleasant and propitious evening for a stroller, what?'

The two men jumped as if someone had shot at them. Annie recognised Mr Clingon, the school bursar. He looked absolutely stunned for a moment. Then he went deep red, and hastily shuffled all the papers he was holding into his briefcase, creasing them up in his rush.

The other man was just as shocked, but a lot smoother. He rose quite calmly to his feet and said, 'Yes indeed. Lovely evening. Are you all set for the new term? All bright-eyed and bushy-tailed, I hope?'

'Bushy-tailed?' queried Sonja, mystified.

'Bright-eyed?' murmured Uem.

'Yes, thank you,' said Annie. She looked pointedly at Clingon's black leather briefcase. There was something deeply suspicious about that shifty-eyed expression. 'Isn't this a strange place to work?' she asked.

'I . . . I . . . that is . . .' spluttered Clingon.

'It was my idea,' said the other man smoothly. 'It's so stuffy on the train, and then to sit in an office when you could be out here among all this . . .' he gestured to the trees around them. 'But talking of trains, I must be off. I'll leave you to the rest of what looks like a perfect late summer evening. Goodbye, Mr Clingon.' He shook Clingon's hand. 'I will be in touch in due course. Goodbye, children. Perhaps we'll meet again.' He strode off down the path towards the river and the road beyond.

Five pairs of eyes plus Lance's fringe were now fixed questioningly on Clingon, who looked very uncomfortable. 'Yes. Indeed,' he said. 'Lovely evening. Well, well. Must be off. Plenty of work to do. Nice to be in the outdoors for once, but it's not wise to make a habit of it, eh? I might try to get up one day and find my feet have taken root in the soil.'

He delivered the line with so little indication of humour that there was a puzzled silence before it was realised that Clingon had cracked a joke. They laughed politely.

Clingon looked pleased. 'Ah-hah,' he said, less nervous now. 'Well, children, I'd love to chat, but goodness me, look at the time. Another day, perhaps. Love to take you through the finer points of the British taxation system, when I have time. Yes. Goodnight, then.' Clingon hurried off, glancing nervously at them as he headed back to the house.

'What was all that about?' asked Carin.

'He is certainly a very strange man,' said Sonja. 'But that is not a surprise. In a place like this, he fits perfectly.'

Annie was relieved that she wasn't the only one who felt that way about her new school. She felt a bit less anxious about settling down as they all headed back to the main school building, stopping on the way for Uem to delight over the croquet lawn, which he had always imagined as a huge field but which turned out to be a small green space in one of the walled gardens.

All through the evening and again the following morning, there was a steady flow of cars, taxis and limousines coming up the school drive, as the children of the rich and famous were returned to their school for the start of the new term. By lunch-time, it seemed, everyone was present. The army of parents and security men had gone. The school security system took over – a system unique to King Arthur's English Academy, as were so many things.

Charles had correctly reasoned that anyone wishing to kidnap, bomb or otherwise interfere with the population of King Arthur's would need motor transport – the distance from the station was too far to walk, particularly if you were laden with weapons. There was a shadowy team of ex-soldiers who were employed as gardeners and cleaners and who doubled as security guards (unbeknown to anyone except Charles and the school bursar, who wrote their salary cheques). The people of the village were also vigilant on the school's behalf. Strangers were scrutinised carefully; unrecognised cars had their registrations checked against the list delivered to the post office each term. Anything suspicious was passed immediately to the village police station, where the sergeant appeared to be fairly dozy but was in fact a highly trained Scotland Yard man, as were two of his constables.

The villagers had entered into the agreement willingly when Charles and Petal had appeared at their neighbourhood watch meeting with the proposition when the school first started.

They were not paid, but everyone knew how much business was brought into the village by the children and by their families' occasional visits to the village. Also, one of the traditions of the school was to hold a cultural festival at the end of the summer term, to which all villagers were invited and at which the local groups got to meet the school community, get autographs and even display their own talents in music, dramatics and art. No one from Morton Gipping had yet been 'discovered' by a famous director or film maker at one of these festivals, but there was always hope. Meanwhile, the festival was a huge, good-natured party with great food and very exciting company, so the villagers were happy to welcome the school into their midst and protected it with great enthusiasm.

The whole school gathered together in the Great Hall for the first assembly of the year. It was an impressive sight: row upon row of smart blazers, clean shirts and, for the most part, cheerful expressions. Uem stood out from everyone else, as usual. He was the only pupil not in school uniform. His father had insisted that the tribal royal robes must be worn, as was traditional in his country. Uem was disappointed not to be dressing up in these very strange English clothes, but he accepted his father's wishes with good grace. He could not, however, resist buying a blazer, which he wore with great pride over the top of his robes.

Up on the stage the members of staff stood, each clad in an academic gown.

'It's spooky,' said Carin quietly to Annie. 'They look like the cast of a Hollywood movie, not teachers.'

Annie nodded. Every teacher was strikingly attractive; every teacher was fashionably and expensively clothed beneath his or her gown, and every teacher sported immaculately combed and styled hair. When they smiled, as they did now at the entrance of the 'Lunatic Lord', their boss, the mass effect of their perfectly straight, white teeth could have blinded someone who got too close.

The headmaster made a short speech of welcome and added the usual stuff about being part of a community, getting the best out of one's education, paying close attention to one's table manners etc.

'I will now hand over to Mr Brandon Leddan, our head of sports and leisure,' said Mr Asquith finally. 'He has some important things to say about drugs. I want you all to listen very carefully.'

Charles sat down. As always, when Brandon was about to speak, he had to quell a surge of unease. Brandon had neglected to mention at interview that he was a fervent but not very knowledgeable socialist. He did not like inherited wealth or wealth generated, as he put it, 'on the backs of the poor and down-trodden working classes.' While Brandon was, generously, OK about the fame and fortune of actors and musicians and the like, since they had at least done something to earn their money, he was very uneasy about the way they let their children adapt to a life of ease and comfort, rather than pointing out the value of making their own way in the world. So his speeches tended to be, at the very least, controversial. Sometimes they were downright offensive.

Brandon did not make a good start, in Charles's opinion.

'Now listen, you lot. Most of you have grown up in families where hard graft doesn't count for much but money comes easy. People who don't graft, don't think. Remember that. And I particularly want you to be very careful about using drugs.

There's a lot of talk about the drugs culture and how difficult it is to resist. I'm telling you – resist it. If your lives are empty because you've nothing to do except take drugs, find a hobby. Play a sport. Do something constructive.

'And watch out for your friends as well. The staff are always happy to listen to what you've got to say. If you think someone's on drugs, you come and let us know. People out there know that people like you are constantly high as kites on whatever they can find, but it's not going to happen here. Anyone found with drugs or alcohol in their possession will be dealt with immediately, by me.'

This was clearly supposed to be a scary prospect, and some of the quick-witted students in the front had the good grace to look suitably worried. Satisfied, Brandon carried on with great gusto. 'The staff are all trained to spot druggies, so don't try it. You're bound to be caught, and the consequences will be very nasty . . .'

The headmaster sighed. Brandon had already wandered away from the content they had agreed earlier. Charles had pointed out, in no uncertain terms, that Brandon was to set a tone of care and concern in his speech this year, and was not to go for the avenging angel style of last year's presentation. Ever since the last cricket season, Brandon's little outbursts at staff meetings had become notably fiercer.

Charles had listened patiently to Brandon's dire warnings that the reason his cricket eleven was so hopeless was that there was so much drug-taking in school that there were no fit pupils left. He had bitten back his own views on why the team had failed to beat anyone, even the younger kids from the village, who had got up a team for the village fayre.

Charles privately felt sure that the lack of success of Brandon's cricket team was due to his perverse insistence on allowing Madame Deviska to remain the honorary captain. It was her responsibility to arrange fixtures, and she was a fervent supporter of the school team.

Madame Deviska, English culture teacher, loved cricket. She had followed all things English from her earliest days as a Transylvanian countess. But there had been no television in Madame's childhood home, and her knowledge of England came from Radio Four, the BBC World Service and her own imagination. She was horrified to discover, upon reaching England, that the 'common and vulgar people', by whom she meant ordinary schoolchildren, played cricket just as often as the cultural elite.

Madame Deviska had insisted on going to every match to cheer on the school team. She also made it her business to raise standards and to ensure that everyone, whether or not they were on the King Arthur's team, dressed and behaved impeccably. People got fed up with her halting the proceedings while she straightened ties, recommended washing powders which would improve the whiteness of various individuals' whites, and reminded people to say please and thank you and use the right cutlery. People resented her horror at the practice of rubbing the cricket ball on your trousers before you bowled. She often interrupted a match by snatching the ball and declaring that the bowler would not have it back until he promised to stop 'this disgusting and degrading practice, which is full of unpleasant connotations and also makes one's trousers dirty.'

The talented cricketers left the team fairly early on, driven by embarrassment, frustration and the taunts of other schools' teams. King Arthur's did not have a huge list of neighbouring teams wishing to challenge them. It was inevitable, thought Charles, that in the end only the more dense pupils, or regrettably those who regarded cricket as a way to miss lessons rather than a pleasurable activity in itself, could be persuaded to join the team.

Charles could not, of course, say that. So he had to let Brandon run his anti-drugs crusade, which was done with great zeal at the start of every academic year, in the hope of protecting the sportsmen and women of the future. Sometimes, as now, his zeal went over the top and he projected the wrong image of the school. This was not acceptable.

Charles coughed, and Brandon flushed as he realised his mistake. Awkwardly, he changed gear in mid-flow about 'the stinking values of the idle rich who had money to waste on unwholesome pursuits.

'Not that we want to scare anyone into thinking we won't be understanding about the problem,' Brandon said suddenly. 'We are a real community here, a family. So if you're worried about drugs, or you can see the tell-tale signs of misuse in friends around you, don't hesitate to come forward. We will do all we can to help. Now, any questions?'

Sonja whispered something into Carin's ear and Carin put up her hand.

'Please sir, can you explain what these tell-tale signs are?'

'Certainly,' said Brandon with confidence. 'You can quite often tell by the eyes – they get sort of dreamy and vacant. Sometimes behaviour becomes erratic. People change moods very suddenly, or may have uncontrollable spasms . . .'

Suddenly the girl sitting next to the pupil who had asked the question twitched. It was not a big movement, but it drew Brandon's eye. The girl was sitting rather limply, but her right hand jerked suddenly. She didn't appear to notice. She stared into space with a vacant expression, her eyes dull and her mouth half open. He realised it was the Chinese girl who didn't speak English. Not Chinese, he remembered – where was it she was from? Just my luck, he thought sourly, to be landed with a druggie who can't even listen to reason because she can't speak the lingo.

After the assembly, as they were leaving the hall, Brandon took Sonja's arm and drew her to one side.

'I want a word with you,' he said sternly.

Sonja smiled and waved at him. She swayed slightly, and looked at him with her eyes only half focused.

Brandon peered closely into her eyes, looking to see if her pupils had dilated. Sonja suddenly peered back, looking into his eyes just as intensely.

'Now look here,' said Brandon, stepping back. Sonja put her head on one side, and gave Brandon a vague smile again.

'I don't believe this,' said Brandon in a low, fierce voice. 'You're fresh off the boat, can't even speak the language and you've managed to find a supply, haven't you? I expect you belong to one of those Chinese Triads that flood the country with the stuff. Well, you listen to me, my girl. Your card is marked. I'm going to be watching you like a hawk.'

Sonja replaced her vacant smile with a look of intense concern. Brandon's tone of voice would make you shudder whether or not you could understand what he was saying, she thought.

'Ah, good, that's rattled your cage, hasn't it? Beginning to get the drift, are we? About time. You can't understand what I'm saying, can you? So you didn't understand all that namby-pamby stuff our Lunatic Lord, the headmaster, makes me say about being understanding and helping with your problems, either. Well, truth is, if I get the slightest whiff of the stuff when I come near you or any of your buddies, you're in for it. I'll be watching you. All the time. Do you hear?'

Carin and Annie had realised Sonja was not with them when they got out of the hall and turned back for her. 'Is anything wrong?' asked Carin, looking at Brandon's red face.

Sonja smiled. 'Mr Leddan was just explaining to me the drugs policy of the school,' she told Carin in flawless English. 'It was most interesting, and if I get the chance to converse with the headmaster in the near future, I will certainly make sure he knows how carefully and explicitly it was explained to me. I think we'd better go now – don't we have a meeting in the leisure complex? Thank you, Mr Leddan. Goodbye.'

'What was all that about?' asked Carin, as they left an open-mouthed, red-faced teacher behind them.

'It was about . . . manners, I suppose,' said Sonja calmly. 'We were just chatting, the way one does. It was a bit one-sided at first . . .'

Carin looked back at Brandon's face, and laughed. 'You did it to him again, didn't you? You are outrageous, Sonja.'

'I couldn't resist. And he was so rude – it is a shame I have come out in the open. It would have been very interesting to see how far he would go in what he says. He does not like the headmaster very much. Now he knows I know what he thinks, he'd better be nice when I decide I do not wish to run round the sports field getting hot and sweaty . . .'

'Sonja, I can't make you out at all,' said Annie. 'One minute you're all prim and proper and demanding good manners, and the next you're the wildest girl I've met in ages.'

'Well, you know we Chinese are supposed to be inscrutable.'

'But you're not Chinese!' said Annie and Carin in chorus.

'Not usually, no,' said Sonja with a smile. 'But as our teachers keep telling us, we can be whatever we want to be with a little effort.'

Chapter 4

*A*nnie and her new friends settled fairly comfortably into school life. They were introduced to the teachers, given their timetables, and told about the after-school activities on offer. The whole group joined the film club. Uem was very taken with the English Culture Society and Lance joined the Natural History Association.

Natalie took up netball and hockey, and surprised them all by becoming netball captain within a week of joining the team. Most of the time, Natalie was like a quiet little mouse, blushing whenever attention came her way and trying very hard to please everyone, even when she didn't agree with what was being said. But out on the sports field, Natalie became someone else. Annie, who had joined the hockey team because team practice fitted in with the television programmes she enjoyed and other interests, was shocked at how competitive Natalie was. She was like an unstoppable little demon, running here, there and everywhere until even her own team begged for her to slow down.

Nancy Willow, the girls' sports teacher, was not a competitive woman. Before joining the school she had lived for some years in San Francisco, and had become involved with a cult there which believed it could predict the date when the world would end: 24 July 1996. Nancy and her fellow-believers had made all the right preparations, had gathered together for an enormous party and a last chance to say farewell to the world out in the desert. They had spent a whole year in contemplation, and then blown every last cent they possessed on the huge celebration which was to be their last pleasure before an unnamed catastrophe obliterated the earth for ever. But July 24 had come, and had gone. The world continued much the same, except for the journalists who drove up in their wickedly polluting cars, and pointed cameras while they asked, smirkingly, what the cult planned to do now. They had no money, nowhere to live – they had sold their mansion to finance the party – and no purpose in life. The cult disbanded and Petal, who knew Nancy's mother, offered Nancy a job at the school.

'Nancy is not quite in touch with the world, it's true,' Petal had told Charles. 'But she works out every day. She knows the rules of most English sports – some, anyway, and she can learn. She's very fit, and she looks adorable in a swimsuit. OK, so she's a little wacky, but she's the right choice for the pupils, I just know it, Charles.'

Charles had felt a deep sense of unease about employing someone that even Petal regarded as being off the wall. But Petal had got her way, as usual. Nancy arrived, settled in, and was soon a much loved member of the school community.

You had to like Nancy, who was the gentlest of people. She hated to think anyone's feelings could be hurt, and refused absolutely to consider any negative thoughts about anybody. If someone missed an easy catch, it was nothing to do with them not concentrating: the wind had suddenly changed direction. No one ever had to do sport unless they wanted to, and people who expressed a desire to beat their opponents, or expressed aggression in any way at all, were regarded with Nancy's own very special look. 'Nancy's look' was well-known throughout the school. It was a heady mix of bewilderment at how people could be so cruel, and mild disappointment that she found herself among such people. She could look at you like that for a long, long time. Quite often, you found yourself giving in because you couldn't bear to stand there any longer while Nancy tried to work out what to do with you.

The picking of teams was a nightmare for Nancy. Why did people always want the good players on their team? What did it matter whether you won or lost? The important thing was to have a good time, and how could you have a good time if some of your team-mates were feeling devalued and unwanted? Nancy wanted teams picked at random, with no captain, just everyone working together. But the sporty students, including Natalie, argued fiercely that this was no way for a sports teacher to behave.

'Of course it's important to have a good time,' Natalie explained to Annie. 'But winning is the most important thing – why would you go to all the trouble of making yourself hot and sweaty, for nothing?'

Annie agreed with Nancy on this one, but thought it best to keep quiet. So she simply watched as every sports lesson turned into a tussle between Natalie and Nancy about how the teams were to be picked. And Natalie almost always won, because Nancy couldn't bear to argue for any length of time. Afterwards, Annie would ask Natalie about what had happened and Natalie, a mouse once more, would blush and say she 'didn't know what came over her.'

Word among the older students was that Nancy was very much admired by Brandon Leddan. Annie only ever saw him being horrible to Nancy, with whom he argued fiercely in public at regular intervals. But the older girls insisted that Brandon was besotted with Nancy, and just had a funny way of showing it. 'Opposites attract,' they said sagely.

Annie had the chance to witness one of these allegedly romantic scenes during a gym lesson one day. Brandon suddenly appeared at the door, which he had flung open with such force that it hit the wall with a resounding thud.

'What the hell is this?' he demanded, striding into the middle of the gym. He waved a piece of paper under Nancy's nose.

Nancy peered at the paper, and sighed. 'It's the netball team for Saturday's match against St Dunstan's College.'

'Nancy, would it be so terrible if the girls won a match now and then?' wailed Brandon. 'You're going to lose horribly with a team like this. Where are Parminder and Jessamine? And where's your captain, for pity's sake? You've left the captain off!'

Nancy said quietly, 'It's time someone else had a turn at being the captain, don't you think? Caitlin has been captain for a long time now . . .'

'Yes, but there's a reason for that. She's your best player!'

If people were like fireworks, thought Annie suddenly, with blue touch-paper for fuses, Brandon would be going up in smoke just about now.

'Nancy, you just can't do this. We'll be the laughing-stock. My lads have a good chance in the Rugby. They've been training like mad. That's what sportsmen and women are supposed to do, Nancy. Your team is . . . well, they're dross, aren't they? So what if the fat and flabby ones want to be in a team? Say no. No way. That's all you have to do. They can take it, you know. I want to be an astronaut, but I'm realistic about my chances. It doesn't gut me that I haven't been asked to go on the next mission to Mars.'

Nancy caught a girl who was beginning to twist awkwardly on the bars and then gave her full attention to Brandon, who turned a deep red.

'Don't give me that look,' he said peevishly. 'You've gone too far this time, Nancy . . .'

'I am so sorry,' said Nancy sweetly. 'How about seven thirty? It's cinema night at the Morton Gipping Village Hall.'

'Fine!' snapped Brandon. 'I'm glad we sorted that out!' He turned on his heel and marched out of the gym.

'Excuse me?' said Shaheela Khan, from Carin's group, as they watched from the sidelines. 'Did I miss the sensible bit of that conversation?'

'I don't think so,' said Carin. 'They must really fancy each other, eh?'

Soon after term started, everyone was handed a leaflet detailing the half-term trips the school was organising for those who were not going home, and at breaktime that morning the air was filled with excited chatter about who was going to do what.

Annie was determined to go nowhere except home to her mum and dad, but the others in her little group decided to choose one they all wanted to go on. They finally settled for EuroDisney. No one had been before. Lance had lived in Florida, quite close to Disneyland, for years, but his parents had always refused point-blank to let him go anywhere so 'frivolous'.

Throughout the term Annie had marvelled at the array of new books and equipment, including her own personal tennis racket and hockey stick, which was beginning to collect under her bed. But the ever-sensible Carin reminded her that the school could spend as much as it liked on this sort of thing, because it would simply be billed to each pupil's parents. Annie remembered the days at Bradford High, when getting a new exercise book was a bit of an achievement and where she and her friends squabbled over whose turn it was to have the textbook. Now that she wasn't there, these things were cute and endearing, and nothing like as annoying as they had been.

Annie threw herself into school life with as much energy and enthusiasm as possible. She was determined to try to have a good time, and conquer the awful hole she felt inside when she closed her eyes and pictured her parents sitting at the breakfast table, or wandering round the market, without her. Home was ordinary, comfortable, familiar. Here at King Arthur's it was like living on another planet. Annie wished she hadn't made any promises to her parents about how long she would stay. She liked her new friends very much, and she was beginning to get used to taking tea with a chimp and going to lessons where she knew more than the teacher about the subject. But almost every day there was some new, unfamiliar and bizarre happening. Annie longed for a bag of chips on the park bench behind the chippy, with Gayle saying she wasn't hungry and then pinching her chips until she had to go and buy some more. You knew where you were with Gayle.

Lance and Annie became good friends as time went on. Annie loved to talk, and Lance was happy to listen and didn't interrupt. Also, they were in the same tutor group. King Arthur's only had forms, where everyone of the same age was together, for subject teaching. Everything else, like registration and House time, and some art and drama activities, was done in tutor groups, with two or three people from every year. It was strange at first, but it meant you got to know a lot more people.

One morning, Lance asked Annie to go with him to the bursar's office. His dad had written to Clingon about the possibility of providing a music studio. They hadn't seen Clingon since the strange meeting in the garden, and Clingon did not seem to remember them.

'So, your father is interested in providing us with a music

studio? Well I must say, um . . .' Clingon looked at the letter from Lance's father, '. . . er, Lance, is it? That is a very generous offer.'

Lance shrugged. 'Tax dodge,' he said.

'Ah. Um, well, hardly a tax dodge, Lance. Let's just say a more creative use of money than simply handing it over to the Treasury, eh?' he beamed.

Lance did not reply: his hair did not even move. Annie knew that he was watching Clingon with a keen interest. Lance was not shy, as people supposed. He enjoyed observing, whether it was the wood-boring or the human species. If that made people nervous, it just made their behaviour all the more interesting to watch.

'Now, what kind of music room did your father have in mind, Lance?'

'Studio,' said Lance.

'Yes. I was rather trying to get at a little more detail . . . in order to estimate costs, bring in professional advice and so on . . . for instance, what would be the purpose of this . . . studio?'

'Music,' said Lance.

'Orchestral? Jazz? Pop?'

Lance shrugged. 'Whatever,' he said.

'All forms of music, then?'

'Guess so.'

'And pray tell me, if you can . . . what would be the difference between the music studio your father has in mind and the excellent music suite of rehearsal rooms and performance centre which already exist at King Arthur's? Not that I'm looking a gift horse in the mouth, you understand. I simply want to ensure your father's very generous gift is put to the best possible use, when he gives it.'

'If,' said Lance.

'Ah, yes. If he gives it. Quite so.' The bursar shifted

uncomfortably on his feet and Annie instinctively looked at her watch. The conversation had been going for just over a minute – that was about average for Lance before people began to show the signs of strain.

'I did not mean to presume that everything was signed, sealed and delivered. However, I'm sure your father has thought things through very carefully before even suggesting the possibility of such a large gift. I expect he consulted with the family?'

'Accountant,' said Lance.

'Yes, yes, of course. Right, then. We're talking about a music studio for . . .'

Lance took pity on him. 'Recording,' he said.

'For making records,' supplied Annie helpfully.

'Ah! The light has dawned. I'm afraid I'm not up on the latest gadgetry available to you bright young things. A recording studio? Well, well. Perhaps we could make an annual school record, eh? Perhaps it would be, as you say, Top of the Pops! A Christmas Number One, even. Capital idea, capital. A huge asset to the school, I'm sure. Now somewhere around here I have just the right information for your father about the American tax benefits . . . here we are.' He handed over a little booklet. 'I think he will find all he needs to know in there. Now, we can arrange everything from this end, he doesn't need to worry. We can find the right people, get estimates, make deadlines . . . all your father has to do is write the cheque, should he decide to go ahead. I will write to him formally, of course, but perhaps you can tell him what I said, in your next letter. I presume you don't often telephone . . .'

'Why?' asked Lance.

'Um . . .'

'He's wondering how you can hold a conversation with

someone who never says more than two words together,' said Annie.

'Not at all, not at all,' Clingon hastily assured Lance. He shot an evil daggers look at the cheeky young girl, who smiled back at him completely unperturbed. 'It's just so expensive to call trans-Atlantic, that's all. Now, Miss . . .'

'Annie. Annie Tompkin.'

Clingon smiled smoothly. 'Now, Annie. What can I do for you? Is your father also interested in sponsoring something? We have a number of small projects . . . I've got a file here . . .'

He turned his back to look through a pile of papers and Annie and Lance beat a hasty retreat.

'He didn't remember us, did he?' said Annie as they walked back to their rooms.

'Dunno,' said Lance.

'Well, I still think he's weird,' Annie insisted, with a determined lift of her chin.

As Annie and Lance approached the main entrance of the school a sleek black limousine drew up and a uniformed chauffeur got out. He tipped his hat to Uem, who strode through the front entrance and into the car.

'Ah, I have been beseeching for you both,' he said. 'I was hoping you would honour me with your belighted presence at a small tea party in my room as soon as classes break themselves? It is my birthday, and my father has sent a splendid hamper to share with my friends.'

'Cool,' said Lance.

'Sounds great,' said Annie. 'I'm always ready for a decent bite to eat – not that I'm complaining about the grub here, mind. It's the best I've tasted.'

'Grub . . . ? I was not aware one was served such delicacies as grubs here?' queried Uem. He shrugged his shoulders. 'I must be away now, if you will please excuse me. I must pick up my hamper and my gifts from the village.'

'Couldn't the post have delivered them here?' asked Annie.

Uem smiled. 'There is one very special gift, and it cannot be brought by post. I will show you, at teatime. Goodbye now. I mean . . . cheerio, what?' he said with a proud flourish. 'Yes, cheerio. You see I am already learning the native style.'

The chauffeur opened the door to the limousine and Uem swept inside, in a flurry of bright, floating cloth.

'Cheerio?' queried Lance.

'My mum says that a lot,' said Annie. 'He must have been talking to someone really old. What is this present, I wonder, that can't be delivered?'

They went off to their physics lesson, taught for the first time by Miss Maloney. She had not been there at the start of the term, as she'd had a small role in a film. The supply teacher, a needlework enthusiast from the village, had not known much about physics, but they had completed some very nice collages.

Miss Maloney was very young and looked somehow fragile. Her pale green eyes were fringed by very dark lashes. Masses of strawberry-blonde hair tumbled in a carefully arranged way on to her shoulders.

Lance was transfixed. He even swept back his hair to get a better look. 'Wow!' he breathed, as Miss Maloney walked past their table and left a delicate scent in the air.

Sonja and Carin exchanged glances. 'Men,' sighed Carin. 'Big eyes, simpering smile, and they're lost.'

Natalie said quietly, 'Yeah, that's right enough.' Her voice was soft but for a moment her brown eyes flashed with anger. Annie knew she was thinking of her stepmother. Natalie had told Annie that her parents had divorced after her father left for another woman, and that she and her stepmother did not get on. She had said no more than that to Annie. Carin, who was in the same tutor group and knew Natalie a bit better than the others, knew a bit more. She had seen a photo of the stepmother and said she looked like a model. But Natalie did not like to talk about home.

There had been a letter from Dublin, Natalie's home town, that morning at breakfast. She had gone red in the face when she read it, and had screwed it up into her pocket without a word.

Miss Maloney seemed to follow the usual school pattern of being very attractive to look at but having no idea how to teach. They were supposed to be doing experiments with lights. Each pair was equipped with a torch, some glass and some coloured paper. 'It's an experiment in refraction,' said Miss Maloney. 'You'll find it on page twenty-two of your textbooks. Now, you can see from the diagrams what you have to do . . .' and so they were left to follow the instructions themselves.

Miss Maloney wandered round the classroom bestowing gorgeous smiles and a light touch on the arm or shoulder here and there. If someone raised a hand and claimed to be stuck, Miss Maloney would look regretfully at the offending child and then simply ask another pupil to explain. Annie wondered if this was a good teaching technique, or if perhaps Miss Maloney did not know the answer herself . . .

When Casey Jenkins started making hand-shapes of rabbits in the shadow cast by his partner's torch, Miss Maloney turned sorrowful eyes on him. 'Oh, Casey,' she said, in a slightly distressed tone. 'Please don't do that.'

He instantly stopped, and turned his attention to the textbook again, scarlet-faced.

'She wouldn't be able to do that at Bradford High,' said Annie with a smile. 'They'd make a mincemeat sandwich out of her.'

'Oh, Casey,' mimicked Sonja, with exactly the breathy, little-girl voice Miss Maloney had used. 'Please don't do that.'

'It is strange, isn't it?' said Carin. 'I mean, none of the teachers exactly teach, do they? Apart from Steph Harvey and that twit of a PE teacher, they don't even seem to know very much about their subjects, never mind how to control a class. Yet all the classes run smoothly, and people are hardly ever rude or disruptive. How can that be?'

'No point,' said Lance.

'He's right,' said Annie. 'They don't need to do anything, do they? If you caused a riot, I bet they would just quietly leave the classroom and let you get on with it. Any damage done to the school would be billed to your parents, and if you were really bad they'd chuck you out. No skin off their noses, with a waiting-list of the rich and famous trying to get into the school. My dad said I only got in because they have to allow a certain percentage of natives. There isn't a waiting-list of Brits – if you live abroad you're far more likely to have heard of King Arthur's than if you live here.'

'Why is that?' asked Natalie.

Annie smiled. 'I expect most boarding-schools thrive on parents who are sending their children as far away as possible.'

Carin and Sonja grinned, but Lance kicked her on the ankle, and jerked his head towards Natalie, who dropped her torch and dived under the table looking for it.

'I didn't mean . . .' Annie was horrified that she might have upset Natalie, even though she couldn't work out how. She dived under the table and the two girls faced each other, on their knees. Natalie had tears on her cheeks.

'Natalie, I'm so sorry . . .'

'There appears to be two children under the table – why is that?' asked Miss Maloney in a tone of gentle despair.

Annie crawled out and stood up. 'We were looking for the torch,' she said, and placed it on the table. 'But actually, Natalie doesn't feel very well. Can we go and get a bit of fresh air?'

'If Natalie is unwell, she must go to the sanatorium and see the nurse,' said Miss Maloney. 'You may take her, if you wish. Now, does anyone understand this bit at the bottom of page twenty-four . . . ?' Miss Maloney turned away.

Annie bobbed down again. Natalie had scrubbed her face with a tissue, and was composed.

'I'm all right,' she said. 'Sorry, I know you didn't mean anything. Actually I am a bit off-colour today. I've had a headache all morning.'

'Well, let's not waste an opportunity to get out of a lesson, eh? I'll come over to the san with you and we'll wheedle a paracetamol out of the nurse, then go back to our room and have a can of Coke or something, yeah?'

Natalie nodded.

They walked across the school grounds and up to the bridge in silence. Halfway across, Natalie stopped and rested her arms on the bridge. Annie joined her, and they watched the water rushing away beneath them.

'Ever play Pooh sticks?' asked Annie suddenly.

'No. What's that?'

Annie searched around. 'It's a game that Winnie-the-Pooh played. You know, the bear in the stories? Here.'

She selected two twigs from the ground and gave one to Natalie. 'Here you go. We race them. When I say go, drop the twig in on this side, and then we watch on the other side to see whose twig gets under the bridge first. Ready? One, two, three, go.'

The girls each dropped a twig and the water instantly swirled around the sticks and carried them under the bridge out of sight. They turned to lean over the other side of the bridge. Natalie's twig rushed through first, followed some seconds later by Annie's, which had been slowed down by a clump of leaves sticking to it.

'It's a daft game, but I used to love it when I was little,' said Annie. 'I drove me mam and dad mad – every time we went for a walk, and saw a bridge, we had to play Pooh sticks.'

'We never went for walks,' said Natalie. She turned her face away.

'Look, Nat, what is it? I mean, I don't want to pry. You just tell me to shut up and mind me own business, but . . . what was all that about, back in class? I don't understand.'

'I really have got a headache,' said Natalie with a weak smile. 'So I was on edge. I know I over-reacted.'

'You don't really believe your dad sent you here to keep you as far away as possible, do you?'

'No, not him. Her.'

'Your mother, you mean?'

Natalie shook her head. 'Not my mother. We never see my mother. When I was six years old, my father met Her. The Ice Maiden, I call her. When I was little, I really believed that she was a witch and she had put some kind of spell on my dad, you know? She is very beautiful but very cold, like snowflakes.

'My mother couldn't bear it, when she and my dad broke up. She went sort of mad. Then she went back to Dublin. For a while, she sent me letters and presents, photographs. I had to stay with Dad and the Ice Maiden, because first of all Mum was in hospital and then they said she couldn't look after me properly. We were travelling quite a lot then. My dad deals in racehorses and studs – you know, he takes really good horses here, there and everywhere, to mate them with mares from a good line of runners.

'In the early days I travelled with him, learning the business so I can take over one day . . . She doesn't like horses much, the Ice Maiden. Says they're smelly and dangerous. But she didn't like me being with Dad when she wasn't there. So she started saying that all the travelling would make me stupid and uneducated, that I would go wild like my mother . . . anyway, she found me a boarding-school nice and far away, in Germany. I hated it.'

'But didn't your mum get better?' asked Annie. 'Couldn't you have gone to live with her, if you were so unhappy being sent away?'

Natalie shrugged. 'She sort of got better. There were lots of promises about coming to get me when she had somewhere to live, and a job. It never happened.'

'Didn't you see her at all?' asked Annie.

'I went over to Dublin a few times for a visit,' said Natalie. 'But my dad didn't like me travelling alone. He always tried to take me. Herself didn't like that, of course. So she said I needed to be settled, and I would never be able to do that while I was being tugged between them and my mother.'

'And your dad fell for that?'

Natalie shrugged. 'My dad is an intelligent man, but he likes the easy life and he tries to pretend bad things aren't happening. When he's with her, he loses himself. It really is like a spell. When she isn't there, we get on so well together. We laugh and play cards, or he plays the piano and I sing. We both love jazz. She hates it, of course. "What's that noise?" she says. "Do stop caterwauling."

'In the end, I was glad that I had boarding-school to go back to. We can't stand the sight of each other. But I didn't like the school in Germany. And then they moved to Switzerland, not far from the German border and only two hours' drive from the school. Suddenly it was convenient for Herself to notice that I was unhappy; she suggested another school. She chose England. Nice little country, England – difficult to get to, not just a little drive across the border. They won't use the Channel Tunnel, you see. Dangerous, she says. Bound to cave in, or get done by terrorists. She doesn't want me popping home at weekends. If she can, she'll even find me somewhere to go during the holidays, so I don't have to go home. Painting holidays in France, skiing in Scotland, mountaineering in Wales – I've done the lot, just because She can't stand Dad and me to be together.'

'That's horrible,' said Annie. She thought of her own mother and father, who had both cried as they saw her off at the station, and felt a great rush of homesickness.

'I'm used to it really,' said Natalie. 'Just now and then, when I'm feeling a bit low, I wonder why my dad lets Herself get away with it, and why it feels like he loves her more than me.'

'I'm sure that's not true,' said Annie firmly. 'He's just caught in the middle, that's all. But you should stand up for yourself, make them take notice, if you're not happy.'

'That's easier for some people than others,' said Natalie. She sighed. 'Come on. One more round of Pooh sticks, eh? Let's stand on the bridge rail, and there'll be a bigger drop to the water. Make it more of a race, yeah?'

They balanced a bit precariously on the wide wooden rail and prepared to throw in their sticks.

'Girls! Stop! Wait! Oh wait; PLEASE, don't do anything hasty . . .'

The two girls turned round to see the headmaster's wife, Petal Butterkiss herself, bearing down on them in a cloud of red and gold chiffon, with long tassled scarves flowing behind her. She was puffing slightly as she reached them, and threw her arms round first Natalie, and then Annie, enveloping each of them in a fierce, tight hug.

'Thank God,' she murmured. 'Thank God I got here in time.'

'I beg your pardon?' asked Annie.

'I know,' said Petal meaningfully, looking deep into Annie's eyes. 'I was watching you talking together as I crossed the field back there. I can sense your pain. But child, this is no way to resolve the turmoil within you.'

'I don't think I . . .' stumbled Natalie, but Petal was already well beyond the reach of the real world.

'Sometimes we feel so fragile, so tossed about on life's stormy sea, that we wonder if our little boat will ever get through the storm and reach the safe harbour. And yet, if we look deep into the darkness, we can see the faint glimmer of the harbour light, and the lantern of the harbour-master as he stands above the raging waters, willing us home. And shall we turn from this into the foaming waters of despair? Or shall we move forward and grasp at this little beacon in our sad and dismal lives? Believe me, girls, there is no despair so deep that you cannot climb out of the pit. In days to come you will laugh at the black night when you contemplated surrendering yourselves to the deep, foaming waters of an early grave.'

Annie looked up at the sky. 'Er, it's actually broad daylight,' she said, 'and the water is only about a metre deep. And we weren't planning to jump. We were playing Pooh sticks.'

'Pooh sticks?' murmured Petal. Then her face softened into a beautiful smile. 'Pooh sticks. Ah yes. Charles showed me. Can I play?'

Before they could stutter a reply, she was up on the bridge rail, stick in hand, scarves flying, squealing, 'Here's mine. Come, girls. Throw in your sticks, and see what fortune befalls . . . may the best stick win!'

Petal insisted on three rounds of Pooh sticks, each time throwing herself a bit more enthusiastically into the swing of the game and each time making Annie a bit more convinced that she would end up in the water, probably pulling the girls with her. When she did finally agree to climb down from the bridge, poor Petal looked like a disappointed child.

'Aren't you two supposed to be in lessons?' she asked.

'We were on our way to the san,' said Annie. 'Natalie has a headache. We were going to ask Nurse Guptah for a paracetamol.'

A shadow crossed Petal's face. 'Paracetamol? For a headache? Oh, my dear, do think very seriously about polluting your body with the chemicals of this modern age. It's far better to take in deep breaths, relax, swim a few leisurely lengths, sleep through the afternoon, following an infusion of larnaca and juniper . . . I am happy to make you some tea with my own hands. Oh, but Charles . . .' she tailed off. She realised, too late, that her husband would be aghast that she was inviting two pupils back to her drawing-room during lessons.

'All of that sounds lovely,' said Natalie politely. 'But I think, just this once, paracetamol will be a bit faster. Perhaps some other time . . . ?'

She said it just to be good-mannered, but Petal seized upon the idea. 'Well, if you have an interest, darlings, I am delighted to share with you the ancient healing arts of the Celtic mystics. You see, it's all to do with diet, exercise, the power of the mind. . .' Her eyes grew dreamy. Suddenly she grabbed Natalie and dug her thumbs, quite fiercely, into the girl's temples. Natalie yelped.

'Let me just find the pressure points,' said Petal enthusiastically. 'Ah, yes, I can feel the tension. Relax, child, and let our life forces combine. Take from me the inner calm and tranquillity I am even now transmitting into your nervous system. Feel the tension ebb away. . .'

Petal moved her thumbs off Natalie's forehead, leaving two dark red prints which Annie could only hope wouldn't turn into bruises. Then she started to massage Natalie's neck with such force that Natalie felt she would choke to death: she couldn't speak, and looked at Annie helplessly, gasping for breath.

'That's wonderful, Mrs Asquith,' said Annie loudly, and took Natalie's arm. 'I can truly say I've never seen anything like it. You could stop now. Why, I think Natalie feels better already, don't you, Natalie?'

Natalie, gasping for air, nodded wildly. Annie tugged her out of Petal's reach. 'We would love to stay and learn more, but we do have to go now,' said Annie firmly. 'Miss Maloney might think we're bunking off lessons if we don't go to the san, so we'll just go and say hello to the nurse. Goodbye – and thanks again.'

'Fruitcake or what?' she asked Natalie as they crossed the bridge, leaving the headmaster's wife waving a vigorous farewell. 'She's going to kill someone one day. Complete lunatic.'

'She's quite a character,' said Natalie, once she had her breath back. 'She hasn't made my headache any better, though. Hey, look! Nurse Guptah is waving.'

Nurse Guptah was sitting in the window seat of the plush, deserted consulting room looking rather bored. She had sterilised all the instruments that she had sterilised and never used the day before. She had counted her supplies of bandages and ointments (she never got the total right first time, but had developed a system of simply counting and recounting until she got the same answer twice in a row). She had walked around the school site hoping to come across a depressed or injured pupil, with no success. Her treatment forms lay unfilled on the desk by the window. Her statistics charts were also rather blank. These showed how many people she had treated at the sanatorium each term, linked to a productivity agreement with the head that her salary would rise if she dealt with more than an average number of cases.

No one had been to see Nurse Guptah since term started, except Jeremy Gordanstone with the sprained ankle. She had managed to hang on to dear Jeremy for three and a half days, making sure he had regular poultices applied to his ankle day and night and restricting him to bed-rest and light reading (no television) to keep shock at bay. In the end he managed to get to a telephone while she was in the bath. He called his father, who telephoned the headmaster and insisted that Jeremy was 'released from captivity' immediately. Nurse Guptah had felt very wounded by this dreadful interpretation of her professional concern for the boy. But for the first day or two, before he had started trying to sneak out of the back door, Jeremy had been lively company. She missed him.

So when Nurse Guptah saw these new patients approaching, she almost whooped with glee. She met them at the door.

'Oh my goodness,' she said, taking each of them by the arm and drawing them into her consulting room just as the fox must have coaxed Jemima Puddleduck. 'Come in, come in. You look awful. So white! I did mention to the headmaster my fears that we were about to be hit by a terrible epidemic of something, and it seems I was right. Look at you. Sit down, and I'll get my thermometer.'

'No, no!' said Annie and Natalie, quite alarmed. They had heard Jeremy Gordanstone recounting his experience in the school sanatorium to everyone, and warning them not to visit the school nurse unless they were deathly ill, or fully mobile.

'Natalie has a little headache,' said Annie. 'We just wondered if you had a paracetamol . . .'

'If you don't mind,' said Nurse Guptah primly, 'I will be the one to make the diagnosis. Now, let's start with your blood pressure.'

Half an hour later, after blood tests for anaemia, urine tests for diabetes, and blood pressure checks 'just in case', the two girls were allowed to leave. Natalie clutched a small strip of four paracetamol tablets, with strict instructions to go back to Nurse Guptah the following day at the same time if she still had the headache. Annie's pleas that she had only been accompanying Natalie, and was in fact in the very best of health, fell on deaf ears and she got the same treatment as Natalie, 'as a preventative measure in case poor Natalie is carrying something infectious.' They only just got away in time before Nurse Guptah turned her attention to the possibility of a day or two's bed-rest and further tests to rule out migraines or a brain tumour.

'She has a very cheerful outlook on life, doesn't she?' said Natalie as they left.

'What shall we do now?' asked Annie. 'We've missed physics, and they'll all be halfway through English culture and tradition. Not a subject I feel in great need of, myself.'

'Nor me,' said Natalie. 'Sure, it rankles with me anyway. Why "English", I'd like to know? The Irish could teach the English a thing or two when it comes to culture . . . but no. We get a lesson in how to quarter your cucumber sandwiches, and what to do with the crusts.'

'Yeah, that was a bit of an odd idea, wasn't it?' said Annie. 'I think she watches too much "Blue Peter", myself. Tell you what, let's go and see if Uem is back from the village yet. We might get a sneak preview of his mysterious birthday present.'

Chapter 5

*U*em was indeed back from the village. When Annie and Natalie knocked on his door there was a curious scuffling sound, and a muffled, 'Who goes there?'

'It's only us,' said Annie. 'What are you up to?'

'Arrest yourselves for one brief moment, if you please,' came Uem's voice, stronger now. 'I am in a state of some dishovel.'

The two girls looked at each other. 'Dishovel?' queried Natalie.

'I've no idea,' shrugged Annie.

When he did finally open his door and wave them inside, Uem looked completely normal. He smiled broadly. 'Do beseat yourselves,' he said. 'And perhaps I can offer you the Coca-Cola?' He swung open the door of a gleaming white refrigerator, obviously new. Inside there were some strange vegetables, packets of various mysterious-looking foods and a couple of dozen cans of fizzy drink.

'Very nice!' said Annie. 'So this is the birthday present, is it? Smart idea.'

'This is indeed the official gift of my father to his son,' said Uem.

'Official gift?' repeated Natalie.

'Indeed,' smiled Uem. Then he realised this meant nothing to his companions. 'In my country, there is the official gift, which bespeaks the status and comfort owing to a royal personage. Such gifts are usually jewellery, chalices, crowns or suchlike. They are for display to the public. Since there is no public to witness such a gift here, the refrigerator seemed the most befitting convenience.'

'So what's an unofficial gift?' asked Annie.

'Such a gift is a more personal item, not shared with the public; such a gift as a mother might give a child.'

'I see,' said Annie. Both girls looked expectantly at Uem, waiting to hear more of his own unofficial gift. He began to look a bit . . . 'shifty', thought Annie suddenly. He's changed his mind about telling us what his other present is.

This, of course, made her even more keen to find out. She looked round the room. Everything seemed just as usual, except for the packaging which had been around the fridge. But when she looked more closely, she saw that one of the large boxes did not appear to have anything to do with the fridge. It had small, regularly spaced holes in it, a bit like the box Annie's cat had once gone to the vet in, but bigger . . .

'You've never gone and bought a dog or something, have you?' she said. 'Surely not even you will be allowed to have a pet that size in your room?'

'A dog? Why would I have a dog?' said Uem. 'The food provided in this place is more than adequate, except that the fruits and vegetables are a little tedious to the eye when encountered so often. I have no need to keep my own livestock – and who would kill it, once I had decided to eat it?'

As his friends' faces contorted with disgust, Uem laughed aloud with delight. 'I think you would say, one point to me!'

'You really had me going there for a minute,' said Annie, and she smiled. 'But I am not distracted so easy. What was in that box, Uem? The one with the breathing holes in it – the one that must have come from a pet shop somewhere?'

Uem sighed. 'Very well. I will impart to you the knowledge of my unofficial gift. But I must swear you to secrecy – we can only tell those we trust. Lance knows, now you.'

'You can't tell us, and not Carin and Sonja,' said Natalie stoutly. 'We go around together too much, and it's not fair.'

'Very well. But no more. Now, are you sure you want to see my gift? You may wish you had not made the request, later . . .'

'Just get on with it, and don't be so dramatic,' said Annie impatiently.

Uem slid on to the floor and his top half disappeared under the bed. He spoke in his own language, so they had no idea what he was saying; his voice was soothing, coaxing. When he reappeared, he had a huge snake coiled round his arms and shoulders. Natalie screamed and took several steps backwards, towards the door. Annie felt frozen to the spot.

'This is Neru,' said Uem. His voice was more gentle than Annie had ever heard it. He sounded like an ordinary boy, rather than a prince who expected to be obeyed wherever he went. 'Say good morning to my friends, Neru. They will not harm you.'

Uem moved closer to Annie. Her knees felt like water. She wanted to move, but couldn't. The snake was looking right at her. She closed her eyes, waiting for the pin-prick of its venom and the end of her life. Nothing happened. She opened her eyes, and found both Uem and Neru looking at her quizzically.

'Do you not like the pythons?' asked Uem. He appeared genuinely surprised.

'Uem, I'm scared witless! Take it away!'

'Scared? But Neru cannot harm you. He does not bite. He kills his prey by crushing them and swallowing them whole. Why would he be interested in you? Neru is a sensible creature. He knows you would not taste good or be easy to digest. He knows you are healthy, and would resist him. If you were sick and slow, then he might be interested in you. Come now, touch his skin.'

Annie took a deep breath and briefly touched the python's body. She expected it to feel cold and slimy, but in fact it was smooth and warm. Still, she removed her hand as carefully – and as quickly – as she could.

'Would you like to take Neru into your own arms and wind him about your person?' asked Uem kindly.

'Er, just about as much as I'd like to eat a pack of razors,' said Annie. 'Let's go one step at a time, eh?'

Annie turned to see what Natalie thought of all this. Natalie had gone: Annie opened the door into the hall and found her sitting against the wall, white as a sheet.

'Come on, Natalie,' she said. 'It's OK. It's not a poisonous snake or anything. Come back in. Come on – someone might see you there and wonder what's going on.'

'They wouldn't be alone,' said Natalie. Very reluctantly, she re-entered the room. Neru had been put on the floor, and was slithering back under the bed.

'He will stay there for much of the day,' said Uem. 'They are not very active, except for when they are hungry. Please do not be frightened, Natalie. I am guttered that you have such fears, and so very apoplectic that I did not think more carefully before making the introductions.'

'Where on earth did you get him?' asked Annie. 'Don't you have to have special licences for creatures like that? And have the school said you can keep him here, in your room? I thought Lindy's chimpanzee was a special concession because her dad said it was part of his research . . .'

'And because he paid full fees for Lynchpin,' interrupted Natalie.

'Yeah. Have you paid fees for this snake? Has this place finally gone so insane that the whole of Bristol Zoo could ship on down here and we wouldn't turn a hair? I suppose we'll be learning French alongside a hippopotamus tomorrow. Why not?'

'I think because a hippopotamus would find it very hard to sit upon a school chair,' said Uem seriously. 'Unless I have the wrong animal in my head picture.'

Sometimes, Annie felt she was the only sane person to be found in the whole school. It crossed her mind that if she let her parents know that wild and dangerous animals were welcomed on to school premises, they would probably tell her to come home at once, and she would not have to stick it out for a year like she had promised.

'Do not besturb yourself,' said Uem. 'I have all the appropriate dockyards.'

'I think you mean documents, Uem,' said Natalie. 'Dockyards is to do with ships.'

'Quite so. Thank you. I have the necessary documents. The headmaster does not know of Neru's presence in his school. I do not think he would allow Neru to become a student, for only yesterday I heard that Damien Gart tried to enrol his Dalmatian hound and was told the animal must stay at home. Lynchpin is an honouroby student, and the headmaster has decreed that there will be only one honouroby student of the animal classes at one time. In any event, my mother has said it would be better not to mention Neru to anyone.'

'She's right. But what about food, and . . . well, exercise?' asked Annie, suddenly wondering if pythons went hunting for their prey. 'How can you keep it a secret?'

'I have bribed the necessary officials,' said Uem calmly.

'Bribed? You've bribed people who work in the school?' exclaimed Natalie, astonished.

'But of course. How else could I be sure of their help and their disrection?'

For Uem, bribery was clearly a part of everyday life. He did not see it as anything more than a bit of gamesmanship.

'Discretion. So, who have you bribed?'

'I have paid Mrs Mungo, the splendid lady who cleans my room. She will not speak of it as long as I give her my most solemn vow that Neru will stay in his box when she comes to clean. One of the kitchen staff will make regular trips to the village for food, and Griggs, the head gardener, will allow Neru the use of the goldfish pond occasionally, as long as he does not consume all the goldfish.'

'And how are you going to stop him?' asked Annie.

'I will make sure he is not hungry when he takes a swim,' said Uem.

Natalie shuddered. 'I don't like it,' she said. 'What do they eat, anyway? Don't you have to keep a supply of dead rats or something?'

Uem weighed up in his mind whether to tell her about the deal he had done with a local farm to supply live day-old chicks. He thought it best to change the subject.

'Pythons are not hard to please,' he said vaguely. 'Now, pray do tell me why you are not in the lesson? I told the teacher that in my country it is considered very rude and vulgar to work on the birthday of any member of the royal family, including oneself. It was very civil of the headmaster and the teachers involved to believe me, and it was a good popportunity to install Neru in his new abode while no other people were present. You are neither royal nor celebroting a birthday. What is happening?'

Annie and Natalie explained where they had been and settled down to enjoy the last ten minutes before the bell went and they ran out of excuses for not being in lessons.

They met up with Sonja and Carin again in French. Annie had hoped to be able to get a quiet word in to warn her friends about Neru, but Monsieur Chevalier was in a bad mood and insisted on silence. 'I think we shall 'ave a test,' he said sulkily. 'Yes, a test on . . . What shall we test today? I think we shall test verbs. Oui, this is good. Out wiz your little notebooks, and we shall test your written knowledge of a language which is far too beautiful to be spoken by these terrible young people wiz their terrible, terrible accents . . . except for you, Madeleine, of course.'

Monsieur Chevalier simpered at Madeleine, who was actually French and only attended French lessons because the alternative was Spanish and that would mean making an effort. Madeleine's Frenchness was one of the school's best-kept secrets. Naturally, she passed all the tests with flying colours, and was Monsieur Chevalier's star pupil. Whenever they needed to impress parents with the school's language skills, Madeleine would deliver a speech in French with just the hint of an English accent, and people would marvel at the brilliant talents of the French teacher, who could train an accent like that, and despair at their own poor clod of a child, who didn't seem to be learning much at all.

Monsieur Chevalier would brook no arguments about the whole point of tests being that you had to have time to revise for them. They all did miserably, except for Madeleine and Natalie and Lance, who had lived in French-speaking countries. Annie had no chance to ease Carin and Sonja in gently to the topic of Uem's new room-mate, who was waiting to greet them, wrapped around Uem's waist and neck, when they entered his room.

Sonja refused, point-blank, to come any nearer than the doorway. But Carin and Lance were very enthusiastic about Neru, and handled him quite confidently. Carin even offered to feed him, but Uem sensibly said it was best done when they had all gone. He was concerned that Natalie, Sonja and Annie might be upset – or even be sick on his carpet – if they observed the feeding ritual of a python. Uem also suggested that when they all met together it would be best to do it in Lance's room. Natalie did not feel this was much better. Lance had several glass tanks with pieces of wood in them being whittled away before their eyes by the tiny creatures who were never actually seen but who managed to demolish wood at surprising speed. But the tanks were firmly closed, on the insistence of the bursar, who had also made sure Lance's father had taken out a special and expensive insurance policy to cover for damage by wood-boring insects, should there ever be an escape. In a school the age of King Arthur's, there was always hope that such a policy could be used to deal with woodworm in other parts of the school, should it be discovered. He would perhaps be able to claim that Lance's special and exotic varieties of wood-boring insects travelled very fast.

Back in the headmaster's house, Mr Clingon was sitting down to afternoon tea with Mr and Mrs Asquith. Charles, who was a very kind and generous-hearted man, found it easy to like a great number of people. But with Clingon, he felt a slight sense of distaste. Perhaps it was because they only ever discussed money when they were together, and Charles had a bit of a horror about money. It was like sex education lessons – embarrassing and often hard to understand. Or perhaps it was because Petal had taken against Clingon right from the start.

Clingon had been appointed to his post because he was by far the best qualified one who applied, and he was not downright ugly like some of the other candidates. But Petal said he had shifty eyes, and that you shouldn't trust a man whose car was bigger than it ought to be.

'If he cares nothing for the environment, why should he care for the traditions of a school?' she had declaimed. Then she had added, a little more shrewdly, 'And how does he afford a big car like that anyway?'

Charles felt he needed to compensate Clingon for not liking him by being especially nice. But with people Charles really liked, he offered protection from Petal's hospitality. When Clingon came to tea, he was content to let Petal take care of the arrangements. Consequently, Clingon was at this moment contemplating the tiny bits of leaf in his dark green tea, with an expression of noble suffering.

'Now, you just make yourself comfortable on the sofa. Ginger cake?' asked Petal. Her eyes glowed with warmth, as though he was a valued guest. She liked to keep her hand in with a bit of acting now and then.

'Ginger cake' conjured up a picture of golden, warm sponge, a little sticky in the middle. Mrs Barton made excellent ginger cake. 'That sounds delightful,' he said. 'Thank you.'

Too late, he saw Charles's regretful shake of the head. Petal handed him a plate with a large slab of something very dark brown on it.

'I made it myself,' she said.

'Ah. Capital. Unusual colour . . .'

'I know Mrs Barton makes it dripping with unsatisfactory toxins. Mine has honey instead of sugar, and no fat at all. All the butter has been replaced by chopped, dried prunes.'

'Prunes? How . . . fascinating,' said Clingon. He looked around the room instinctively, as he had done as a boy when his mother insisted on feeding him spinach or liver. Was there no conveniently placed bin, flowerpot or drawer he could reach, if a slight diversion could be made?

'Yes. Prunes are a very good substitute for butter, and so much more in tune with your body's requirements. This is a recipe from the United States. I've never come across it here in England.'

'Well, isn't that strange? Such an interesting idea . . .' Petal was watching him expectantly. He took a bite, as small a bite as he decently could, and laid the slab back down on the plate. There was an audible ringing sound as it made contact. 'Yes, you can certainly taste the prunes,' he said politely.

Petal, satisfied, went to 'refresh the pot' by throwing a few more nettles into the tea. Charles wrapped his piece of cake in his napkin and placed it in his pocket. 'I'm saving mine for later,' he smiled.

Clingon, relieved, did the same. 'Quite. Capital. Now, here are the accounts and financial predictions for the next quarter. As you can see, I have computed the capital gains against losses made in the two previous financial years, aggregated the ten per cent wear and tear adjustment for the next financial year and costed three options for the covenanted income and special project finance . . .'

He talked very quickly, and soon he could see a slight glaze over Charles's eyes. After a further couple of minutes it was clear he had lost the headmaster completely.

'So that's the position,' he finished. 'As soon as you sign the appropriate documents I can contact the school accounts auditors and have everything tidied up.'

He thrust a sheaf of papers over to Charles, sheets of closely typed, small print documents. 'I have marked with a cross the places requiring a signature by tomorrow. You might wish to read over them tonight and discuss it further, of course . . . you need to be sure I'm not cheating you, after all.'

Charles laughed with him. 'I'm sure the auditors would tell me if they found you living a lavish life-style on the proceeds of school funds,' he said jokingly. He signed the papers as Petal re-entered bearing the refreshed pot.

'Good. Now I must be on my way,' said Clingon hurriedly, eyeing the teacup still half-full of cold nettle tea. 'Never a dull moment in school finance, eh?'

He gathered up the papers and left. Petal watched him go with a malevolent eye, repeating with some pride the look she had developed for her role as the Snow Queen in Boston. She had been nominated for an award. 'I don't trust that man, Bunny Beaver,' she said, for the hundredth time. 'And whatever he wants you to do, you should say no until you have consulted someone else.'

'Petal, you distrust him because he is pale, and has small eyes, neither of which he is in a position to change. I do think it's a bit hard to write a man off because he isn't handsome enough, my darling. He is a talented accountant, who came to us highly recommended.'

'Hmm.' Petal, unconvinced, turned to cutting her husband another piece of ginger cake which she would watch him eat; it made her proud to see him enjoying her cooking.

Clingon, reaching the privacy of his office, grinned with satisfaction and reached for the telephone. 'Hello? Yes. No problems. Didn't even read it – don't worry, I know how to handle him. Yes, that's right. Blue Dolphin, eight o'clock, Wednesday. I'll meet you there.'

Chapter 6

*I*t was Uem who decided that they should all join the King Arthur Dramatic Society.

'It is an essential requirement of the experience of English culture for which our respected and veneered parents are paying considerable sums of money,' he told the others. 'One cannot avoid the amity dramatic if one is to say one has truly experienced the English education. Indeed, it will become fun and very uplifting, to be embroidered together in a joint undertaker of such importance to the local community.'

'Embroidered?' queried Sonja. Lance shook his head. Usually you could have a good guess at which word Uem had muddled with another, but sometimes he completely baffled them all. They had got used to listening to the basic idea of what Uem said, and not taking much notice of his attempts to use as many words as possible. Uem loved the very different rhythm of all those English words strung together and felt it was an insult to the language to speak too few of them.

Once Uem had decided they would join the dramatic society, there was no point in arguing. He was very polite, very charming, but relentless. He was also used to being obeyed, and found it genuinely confusing when people didn't fall in with his wishes.

'He tries so hard not to boss us about,' Annie wrote to her mother, 'that you feel sort of duty-bound to give in to his coaxing as often as you can, just to encourage him. And so it is that when you come to collect me at the end of this term, you'll be treated to the sight of your only child dressed in a weird frock, prancing about and saying, "Aye, my Lord!" a lot.'

This was not how Letty Domingo described the production, of course. In the same post as the letter from Annie, Mr and Mrs Tompkin received a glossy invitation to 'Scenes from Camelot: An Interpretation of the Arthurian Legends' where Annie's name appeared on the cast list as 'second lady courtier'.

Letty felt Annie had considerable dramatic talent, and would have offered her a larger part, but Annie had offended Petal Butterkiss, who was directing the show. At the audition, when Petal had been trying to show them the deep-breathing techniques that would allow them to unlock their Inner Beings and join the Ancient Forces of the Natural Elements, Annie had laughed. This had set everyone off, and what had been intended as a truly spiritual awakening of the forces of creativity had become a schoolchild's farce. So Letty's suggestion that Annie be considered for a more major role had fallen on deaf ears.

Petal and Letty had drawn up quite a demanding rehearsal schedule for the main characters, and Uem, who was to play Sir Gawain, threw himself into preparations for his role with enormous enthusiasm. His father had promised to pay for all the costumes needed in the production, and Uem had immediately gone out and bought a full suit of armour which stood in his room already, awaiting the dress-rehearsal. Neru had taken quite a shine to the armour and hid inside it in the warm darkness as often as he could. Letty had tipped Petal off before auditions that giving Lance a speaking part probably wasn't a good idea, since no one actually knew if he could speak more than two words at a time. So he had the part of the village idiot. He was brilliant, and played the part without any words at all. His arms and legs became gangly almost before their eyes, and he stumbled, and dribbled from underneath his hair, with just enough energy to be convincing.

'He knows about communicating without words, of course,' said Carin sagely. 'That's what makes him so good.'

Carin and Annie had minor roles and said a few lines each: both agreed that medieval ladies were feeble, wimpish creatures and they were glad they weren't alive in those days.

'How could they just stand there and let a load of men decide how they would live their lives?' said Annie. 'The great and legendary King Arthur deserved a slap in the chops sometimes, if you ask me.'

Sonja refused point-blank to consider any of the female roles for this very reason. Petal, having watched the range of her facial expressions and amazing gift for mimicry at audition, was all for having her cast as Guinevere. But Sonja wanted to be one of the knights.

'My dear, only think,' said Petal, trying to be tactful. 'You are . . . well, as I am sure you know, you are a rather striking-looking girl.'

'But small,' said Brandon, who had volunteered for stage manager.

Sonja looked at him angrily, and he smiled. Point to Brandon, he thought. Little madam.

'It's wonderful to be small, of course,' said Petal desperately, wishing Brandon would go and plug something in, and leave her to deal with the situation. 'Especially if you're a woman. But knights were . . . bigger. Next to Uem, you would not be terribly convincing, my dear.'

'You'd look like a ventriloquist's dummy,' said Brandon, laughing so hard he could hardly spit the words out.

Petal took Sonja's arm and turned her away from Brandon. 'You would look so wonderful as Guinevere. I have a lovely shot silk gown in just your size. We could give you a long blonde wig. With your skin colour you would look . . .'

'Freaky,' said Sonja, aghast.

'Symbolic,' said Petal firmly. 'Impossible compositions. Don't you see? Lancelot and Guinevere. China and England.'

'What exactly does China have to do with this?' asked Sonja. Her voice was icy. Annie flinched on Petal's behalf.

'I . . . but my dear . . . Mr Leddan told me you were a Chinese refugee . . .'

Another point to me, thought Brandon. He made a diplomatic exit to check the spotlights. Sonja, once she had calmed down and agreed not to poison Brandon's tea at the first possible opportunity, was persuaded to stay in the production as a beggar child. She adamantly refused to take on a speaking part despite Petal's pleadings.

Petal wanted the cast to 'bond together', and invited all the students involved in the production for tea at the headmaster's house. Charles, out of sympathy for them, tried to persuade Petal to let the school caterers take care of the food, but Petal felt it ought to be made with her own hands.

'Food is a love offering, a symbol of service,' she told Charles. 'If I as the director humble myself into the role of servant and provider of food, I will be able to extract the very best performance from each individual. No, Charles, I think it's very sweet of you to worry about me getting too tired, but this is a sacrifice in the cause of Art, and I am willing to make it.'

Consequently the friends, who had missed school tea in order to attend Petal's event, came back to their rooms very hungry, except Uem. He had manfully eaten a sample of everything Petal had offered him, much to her delight. But he had had to chew very hard and for a long time before his stomach would accept the possibility that the foul-tasting substances in his mouth could be going anywhere near it. His jaw ached, and he was very thirsty, but the thought of any kind of food at all made him feel decidedly wobbly. He went off to his room, leaving the others to gather together whatever food they had.

'If I was at home now, I'd be making a toasted cheese sandwich,' said Annie mournfully, surveying the half-eaten chocolate bar, three bags of crisps and two packets of plain biscuits they had pooled.

'I would kill for a plate of bacon and crusty bread,' sighed Natalie.

'Fries!' said Lance with longing.

They surveyed the food in front of them in silence. Hungry as they were, they could not help feeling they deserved better than this.

'I know,' said Carin suddenly. 'Let's go out for a meal.'

Sonja looked at her watch. 'We're not allowed into the village after eight o'clock on week nights. And it's such a tiny place, we're bound to be seen.'

'So we don't go to Morton Gipping,' said Carin. 'We go into town. I'll order a taxi to pick us up at the bottom of the road, so we won't be seen from the school, and we'll go and have a feast somewhere.'

'It will be against school rules,' said Sonja anxiously. 'If we are caught . . .'

'Then we say how very sorry we are, and how we won't do it again, and what will they do? They're hardly likely to expel us for something like that – particularly if Lance comes. They haven't got the money for the recording studio yet.'

'I think Mr Asquith will be very sympathetic,' said Annie with a smile. 'I notice he didn't eat any of his wife's baking himself. And when he saw me stuffing an arrowroot and garlic sponge cake into his potted plant, he looked away and pretended he hadn't seen anything.'

'Do you think that's why he was so fidgety all evening?' asked Natalie. 'I thought he was very shy – but maybe he was embarrassed, because he knew how disgusting the food was.'

'Well, then. Are we going or not?' asked Annie. 'We all have to be in our rooms for last registration soon, so we need to decide.'

'I vote for getting a taxi for eight thirty, after Nurse Guptah's round. We won't be able to eat until nine, but at least we'll have something worth waiting for. A couple of biscuits just won't do for me, I'm afraid,' said Carin.

'I would rather not risk trouble,' said Sonja. 'I will eat the biscuits, if I may, and stay here. Uem might be ill, after all – he ate quite a lot of that food. I will check later that he is well.'

'I'll stay too,' said Natalie. 'If we are caught, they might write home. The Ice Maiden would just love for me to get into trouble, and she'd use it against me somehow. I can't risk it. Sorry.'

'Well, I'm in,' said Annie. 'Lance?'

Lance shrugged his shoulders. 'Sure.'

'Right,' said Carin. 'I'll go and order a taxi. Tell you what – we'll see if we can get something to bring back for the others.'

They went off to their rooms for the goodnight ritual. At eight o'clock Nurse Guptah started her rounds. She ticked everybody off on the register, carefully scrutinising for flushed faces, or bumps and scratches that might need medical attention. She prided herself on saying goodnight to each pupil personally, so that they could bring to her attention anything that was worrying them. If nothing was worrying anybody, she would dig a bit deeper. It was best to take it in turns to have some kind of problem which Nurse Guptah could easily sort out – a minor scratch, perhaps, which she could bathe in TCP and put a plaster on, or a spot which would enable her to give out leaflets and sage advice on skin care. Saying goodnight was a time-consuming business at King Arthur's.

Finally, Nurse Guptah moved on from their wing, having advised Natalie that a cucumber poultice would be very good for the shadows under her eyes. Annie and Carin called for Lance and went downstairs. The hall was deserted, the side door unlocked for staff and pupils who had applied for late passes. Manfred was on duty this week, and he was at an intricate stage with one of his engines, so his patrols were a little less frequent than they should have been. The three got out without any trouble, and ran down the road to the waiting taxi. Carin had sensibly ordered it from a large company in town, not from the village where the local driver might ask questions.

Once in town they walked around the centre, looking at the menu boards. Only the Blue Dolphin offered something for everyone ('Best fries,' pronounced Lance, peering through the window at people's plates), and they were seated at a quiet table by a bank of silk trees and shrubs.

'Not easily seen from the road,' said the waiter, smiling. 'So, tea with the headmaster's wife, was it?' This wasn't the first time King Arthur's students had sneaked into town. He wondered what Petal Butterkiss had offered up this time.

After they ordered the food, Annie sat back and surveyed their fellow diners. Wednesday was a quiet night for restaurants, but more than half of the tables were occupied. There was something familiar about the two men sitting near the window at the front . . .

'Oh no!' breathed Carin at the same moment. 'That's Clingon, isn't it?'

'Yep,' said Lance cheerfully.

'Did he see us come in, I wonder?' asked Annie.

'Nope,' said Lance.

'Are you sure?'

'Yep.'

'Who's that with him?' said Carin. 'Isn't it the man from the garden? That one you said was shifty, Annie?'

'Yes it is,' said Annie grimly. 'One meeting in the garden, where we caught them. Now they have one at a hotel well away from the school – perhaps the two are connected, eh? Maybe they're meeting here because we caught them. What are they playing at?'

'Crooks,' said Lance.

They watched the two men, who were talking very seriously. Spread over part of the table were some documents: from time to time Clingon pointed to something on one of them, or scribbled a note.

'We need to see those papers,' said Annie. 'But how? I don't suppose anyone lip-reads, do they? We could at least keep up with the other man's half of the conversation, since he's facing us.'

Carin and Lance both shook their heads. 'Perhaps Clingon has business interests that have nothing to do with the school,' said Carin sensibly, 'and so he doesn't like to use school premises for his meetings. There doesn't have to be a sinister explanation, Annie.'

'Yes there does. There's something definitely fishy about our school bursar,' said Annie. 'I've got a feeling in my bones about him. My dad says always trust your instincts.'

Just then the food arrived. They ate slowly, keeping watch on the two men, who were now concentrating on their desserts and not talking very much.

'If only we could see those papers . . .' said Annie in frustration.

Suddenly Lance put down his fork and stood up.

'What's the matter?' asked Annie.

'Wait,' said Lance, and he strolled off towards the kitchen, hands in pockets.

'Do you think he knows that isn't the done thing in England?' asked Carin. 'If he wants to compliment the chef on his chips, he should do it through the waiter . . .'

But Lance was not thrown out of the kitchen. He was gone a few minutes, and then he strolled back to the table and picked up his fork.

'What was all that about?' asked Annie.

Lance smiled. 'Watch!' he said.

The waiter was bringing a tray of coffee to Clingon's table. Expertly he set down the coffee pot, the cream jug, the cups and saucers and the sugar and murmured something to Clingon. As the waiter picked up the water jug and glasses to put them on the tray, one of the glasses overbalanced. It was half full of water, and it tipped all over the papers lying on the table.

Clingon sprang up – some of the water had clearly gone on his jacket. The waiter was profusely apologetic and said something to Clingon, indicating the papers. Clingon gave him three or four sheets, and the waiter hurried off to the kitchen with them, leaving another waiter to mop the table and apologise again for his colleague's clumsiness.

'Stay here,' said Lance, and off he went to the kitchen again. Two minutes later he was back.

'Well?' said Annie eagerly. 'I imagine that little incident with the water was your doing, was it?'

Lance nodded. 'Yep.'

'How did you get the waiter to deliberately spill something?' asked Carin. 'He could have got into trouble.'

'Money,' said Lance calmly.

'So the waiter took the papers off into the kitchen to dry

them – and you've seen them?' Annie asked.

'Yep.'

'OK, Lance, don't keep us in suspense any longer. And I'd be grateful if you could pretend you were talking about your beloved wood-boring insects, and speak to us in whole sentences!'

Lance sighed, and pushed away his plate. He leaned his elbows on the table, moved his hair out of his eyes and said, 'It's real serious. I didn't get to see all the sheets, but it's some kind of fraud.'

'What did you see?' asked Carin.

'Figures and names, is all,' said Lance. 'School's name's there, plus others. Then there's a list of weird phrases, and a load of numbers beside each one. One of the things was Rosy Dawn, another was Packing it Pretty – real weird stuff.'

'They sound like horses' names, don't they?' said Annie. 'But there's no reason to keep having a little flutter on the gee-gees a big secret – unless he's using school funds. Maybe he's a compulsive gambler.'

'No,' said Carin. 'He's not the type. He's a control freak, if anything. He wouldn't lose his head and risk money on a horse. Clingon's an accountant through and through. If he does something, it's because he's calculated a certain profit. Doesn't fit with the bookies.'

'So what do you think is going on?' asked Annie.

Carin shrugged. 'No idea. We need more information.'

'I don't think your water trick is going to work twice,' said Annie grimly. 'What do we do? Should we tell the headmaster or someone that his bursar might be on the fiddle?'

'No proof,' said Lance, slipping back into his usual self.

'We have no proof of anything except a bit of strange behaviour,' said Carin. 'And we are talking about a member of

King Arthur's English Academy, remember. Find me three people who are not behaving a bit oddly, apart from us, of course, and I'll buy you a holiday in Timbuctoo. All we would do is let the headmaster know that we were in town when we were supposed to be in school. We will look like the deceitful ones, not him.'

'Look out – they're leaving!' hissed Annie.

They all bent their heads down over their plates. Fortunately the plants screened them, and the men didn't look their way.

'I just know he's up to something,' said Annie. 'OK, so I've no idea what, but tomorrow we need to work out how we can get our hand on those papers for a bit longer. We need a better look.'

'Don't you think we should follow them?' asked Carin.

'There's no point,' said Annie. 'They've had their meeting – they'll split up now, and I bet they've got cars.'

'What shall we do now, then?' asked Carin.

'Eat,' said Lance, picking up his dessertspoon.

They arrived back at the school just after ten thirty, clutching a brown paper bag with bread and ham and cheese from the late supermarket for the others. Too late they realised that getting back into school was not going to be as easy as getting out: it was later now, and although they got into the school grounds, Manfred had locked the side door. A note said to ring for attention.

'Whoops!' said Annie. 'I suppose we either own up and take the consequences, or spend the night in the garden. Which do you fancy?'

'Neither one,' said Lance. He looked up at the windows. All were shut tight. He set off round the corner of the building. Carin and Annie followed miserably.

'Bingo,' said Lance, pointing upwards. A window was open.

'Whose room is it?' asked Annie nervously.

'Storeroom,' said Lance.

'Are you sure?' asked Carin.

'Nope,' said Lance. He grabbed hold of the thick ivy which grew up the walls and started to climb. Lance climbed as lightly and carefully as a monkey, and clearly had lots of experience. He was full of surprises. He disappeared through the window. Carin and Annie stood looking up at the darkness, waiting for him to reappear. Nothing happened. No sound, no lights. Annie hoped this was a good sign – if it was someone's bedroom, there would surely have been a scream and lights – but on the other hand Lance could still be floundering around in the darkness, wondering where he was.

A hand on her shoulder made Annie jump, and she nearly screamed herself. 'Hi,' whispered Lance in her ear.

He had found his way easily in the darkness and opened the door for them. Of course, thought Annie, that thick curtain of hair over his eyes all the time must have given him a lot of practise at seeing in the dark . . .

They crept into the hallway. Night-lights bathed the building in an eerie glow. Everything was quiet. They crept up the stairs and down the first landing, past the rooms where pupils slept or read by lamplight: there was no official bedtime at King Arthur's but there was a requirement to be quiet by ten o'clock on school nights.

Natalie and Sonja were waiting for them and fell upon the contents of the brown paper bag – they were starving. While they ate, Annie filled them in on what had happened at the Blue Dolphin. They all agreed it was a bit of a strange circumstance even for King Arthur's, but they couldn't work out what Clingon could be up to.

A knock at the door startled them all. Lance headed for the cupboard.

Annie went to the door and pulled it open a crack. It was Uem, in red brocade pyjamas and a matching nightcap. 'Are you decently attired?' he asked. 'I wonder if I might impose upon you. I have suffered a serious mishap.' He looked really anxious.

Annie threw open the door. 'Come on in,' she said. 'We're only just back from the restaurant.'

Lance emerged from the cupboard and sheepishly threw off the clothes he had been hiding behind.

'What's the matter?' asked Sonja.

'It is Neru,' said Uem. 'I fed him tonight as is my usual custom, and prepared myself for the sleeping. Unfortunately I had left my book, a fine volim of Shakespeare's sonnets – downstairs in the liba-rory. I went to retrieve it so that I might improve my mind further before retiring to my slumber . . .'

'Get to the point, Uem – what happened to Neru?'

'I do not know,' said Uem in despair. 'I closed the door behind me, but alas not firmly enough. When I returned from the liba-rory the door to my bedchamber was half open. Neru has vanquished!'

Chapter 7

A thorough search of Uem's room began. Everyone joined in, except Natalie and Sonja. They flatly refused, on the basis that they might be the ones to find the creature. They remained huddled together in their room with the door and window shut tight.

There was no sign of Neru. The doors on to the corridor were all shut, for which Annie breathed a sigh of relief. But then she realised there was a fire door at the end of each hallway, before you got to the stairs. These heavy doors automatically swung shut behind you when you went through them. How could Neru have gone anywhere, unless it was into someone's room? The thought of creeping into other people's bedrooms in the middle of the night to search them was not a prospect that pleased her at all. Still less did she want to contemplate the possibility that someone had opened their door and accidentally let Neru in. Any moment now there would be a terrified scream . . .

Lance had padded off down the corridor and returned, pointing back over his shoulder. 'Open,' he said.

Sure enough, someone had propped the fire door ajar, probably one of the staff struggling to get the industrial vacuum cleaner through.

'He must have gone down the stairs,' Annie hissed. 'I hope so, anyway. At least there are no bedrooms down there. Imagine waking up in the middle of the night to find Neru snuggled down beside you.' They all laughed nervously. 'He can't have got far. Come on, let's find him before Manfred does.'

They tiptoed along the hall and crept down the dimly lit stairs, eyes and ears alert for any sign of the snake, or for Manfred, who would patrol the building and immediate grounds until well after midnight.

'We'd better split up,' whispered Annie, surveying the long corridors and open doorways with dismay. 'Howsabout Lance and I go to the left, and you two go to the right. Hopefully the fire doors down here will be closed, so he can't have gone too far. Stick together, and we'll meet back here when we've searched the ground floor. Yes?'

The others nodded, and the two pairs set off in opposite directions. The library door was open a little, and Lance and Annie slipped inside. Softly they shut the door and switched on one of the desk lamps. The book-lined walls glowed softly. Clusters of tables and chairs, computer terminals and magazine racks stood silent. Trolleys and crates for returned books, old magazines and various projects stood tidily against the wall by the librarian's counter. Posters of authors and characters from books smiled down in ghostly satisfaction at their predicament. There were loads of nooks and crannies just the right size for a python who could curl himself up into any dark corner. If he was asleep, he might not take too kindly to being disturbed...
Annie shuddered. 'If he's come in here,' she said to Lance, 'it could take us all night to find him.'

Lance didn't answer. He simply sighed, and started the search.

They worked in silence, taking one side each and working towards the far end of the library. Lance turned another desk lamp on as they moved. Their senses were stretched taut, eyes and ears alert to the tiniest sign of disturbance. They heard Manfred approaching the library before he even turned the handle on the door, and both dived for cover. Annie scrambled under the librarian's counter, nestling into the shelves underneath.

'Hello? Who is in here?' Manfred called. His voice echoed round the library. Annie shrank back into the counter, holding her breath. She shut her eyes instinctively, as if not being able to see anything herself would somehow make her invisible to Manfred as well.

'These students are so careless,' muttered Manfred. 'They leave lights on all the time.'

'Never mind them.' The female voice took Annie by surprise; she had thought Manfred was alone. 'Come on, Mannie. You should be off-duty soon, and I want you to walk back with me. I'm scared in the dark on my own.'

'You have me to protect you, you have nothing to fear,' said Manfred, in his best all-action hero voice.

There was a slight 'Mmm' sound as their lips met, and a sigh of 'Oooh, Manfred.'

Annie froze in horror and shut her eyes even tighter. The woman's voice was vaguely familiar, but Annie could not place it. Whoever the woman was, she would not like to discover that she and Manfred were being observed. Annie had never felt so embarrassed. How far should she let things go before she made it clear to Manfred and his friend that they were not alone?

Fortunately she was saved from this dilemma as Manfred and the woman left the room. On his way, Manfred switched off both the lamps. The library was left in total darkness. Annie and Lance waited in silence for a few moments after they had heard Manfred's weighty footsteps die away.

Annie opened her eyes. It made little difference: the curtains were always drawn at the end of the day, and there was not the smallest chink of light. 'Lance, where are you?' Annie hissed.

'Here,' said Lance. His voice came from the other side of the library.

'Are you near a lamp?' asked Annie.

'Nope. You?'

'I'm not sure,' said Annie. 'I'm sort of in the librarian's counter bit. There must be a switch somewhere, I should think.' She spread her hands over the floor and up the side of the counter, searching with her fingers for any sign of a switch, socket or electric flex which would indicate a lamp. She had been sitting scrunched up in a ball. Now she moved on to her knees. She felt a slight movement behind her; Lance must have found his way over from his hiding-place. He was also searching for a light switch. She felt the slight pressure of his weight as he leaned over her legs and brushed against her waist.

'Lance, get off. That's me you're crawling on.'

'What is?' said Lance. In the same moment that Annie realised his voice was still coming from the same spot – in other words, he was not anywhere near her – Lance found a switch for the overhead strip lighting. Blinking in the sudden glare, he saw Annie on the other side of the library. She was on her knees at the side of the librarian's counter, frozen in horror, with her mouth open as if to scream but with no noise coming out. With one coil wrapped neatly round her waist, and his tail across her legs, Neru was making his way upwards in a neat spiral towards the top of the desk, around Annie's neck.

Annie took a deep, sudden breath.

'Stay calm,' said Lance. 'Don't scream. Annie, don't scream. Don't . . .'

Annie let out the loudest scream ever heard at King Arthur's before or since. Then she screamed again, and again.

Neru, confused at this sudden noise, slithered away to search for a more peaceful companion and Annie collapsed into a heap. Upstairs, there were sounds of doors opening and muffled shouts. Then suddenly the fire bell went off.

Lance had reached Annie now, and he put his hand firmly over her mouth. 'Sssshhh,' he hissed in her ear. 'It's OK. He's gone.'

Annie turned and clung on to him as if she were drowning, almost choking him. Lance watched regretfully as Neru slithered into the stock cupboard – it would take forever to find him in there. But he realised that his first priority had to be to get Annie out of the room.

Lance guided Annie over to the door. Her knees were like water, and she could hardly walk. The whole building was in uproar. The fire bell rang insistently, and a siren could be heard in the distance.

Carin and Uem ran up to them. 'You found him then,' said Carin with a grin. 'We knew you must have, when we heard that scream. Where is he?'

Annie pointed a trembling finger back into the library, and Lance closed the door firmly. 'Stock pile,' he said to Uem.

'He was going to crush me . . .' said Annie faintly.

'He was not!' snorted Lance. 'You were warm, I guess. He was just . . . making contact.'

It was rare to hear a complete sentence from Lance, but Annie was in no state to be impressed, or to comment as she usually would have done.

Carin had her arms around Annie. 'You'd better get in there and find him,' she said to Uem. 'But wait a few minutes – someone will be round to check the rooms.'

'Fire!' said Annie, suddenly coming back to her senses and realising what the awful ringing sound and all the commotion upstairs must be about. 'Oh my God, fire!'

'Relax,' said Carin with a grin. 'Fire *bell*, is all. When I heard you scream, I knew someone would come running to find out what was going on. Since we happened to be standing right by the fire bell, I thought a diversion would be appropriate.'

'Neat,' said Lance.

'Except, of course, that I had forgotten that buildings like this have their fire bells automatically linked to the local fire station,' said Carin. 'So we'd better get away from here quickly. Come on.'

They slipped out of the side door, ran around the building and joined the crowds of pupils assembling on the lawn. There was a buzz of excitement as everyone looked eagerly up into the sky for the tell-tale signs of smoke and flame. Three fire engines swept into the drive and the fire crews jumped out. Teachers clutching registers were calming the more hysterical ones and trying to get people to stand still in their lines so they could check off their names.

'Everybody listen!' shouted the headmaster through a megaphone. In this situation, where he genuinely believed people could be in danger, he cared nothing for image or being everyone's friend. 'You know the fire drill,' he boomed in a very headmaster-type voice. 'Keep quiet, and line up. The fire officers will have to search the building and the staff will have to make sure everyone is out. Therefore it is imperative that you all keep QUIET!' His voice suddenly boomed, and a shocked silence fell. 'That's better. If someone is calling out, we need to be able to hear. Now stay exactly where you are, in silence, until I tell you to move.'

The floodlights had been put on and everyone looked pale and odd, swathed in dressing-gowns and nightclothes. Some of the younger ones had teddies, which they tried to conceal so that no one would know they were at all frightened.

'Well, it seemed like a good idea at the time,' said Carin. Taking a deep breath, she walked up to Mr Asquith. He bent his head to listen as she said something quietly in his ear, then he had a hurried consultation with the fire officers. The leading fireman got out his radio. He said something to Carin, who hung her head, and then he summoned his colleagues back to their engines and they all drove away, leaving a buzz of excited chattering pupils on the lawns.

'Right,' said Mr Asquith through his megaphone. 'It seems this time it was a false alarm. We'll count tonight as an exercise and we'll all learn from it, I'm sure. This just goes to show how important fire drill is, doesn't it? Well done, everybody. Off you go now, back to bed. Thank you very much. Staff, can you meet briefly with me tomorrow morning in the staffroom before first lesson? Thank you, everyone. That's all.'

Everyone trooped off back to their bedrooms, and Uem slipped into the library, with Lance hovering outside the door as lookout.

Annie and Carin found Sonja and Natalie and headed back to their room. 'What on earth happened?' asked Natalie. 'Where was the fire?'

Carin explained that she had set off the fire bell to divert attention away from Annie screaming. 'Of course, I forgot that it would automatically summon all the fire engines,' she said miserably. 'It was a stupid thing to do. What if there had been a fire somewhere else, while all the engines were here? I would never have forgiven myself.'

'There wasn't another fire,' said Natalie. 'And they didn't look exactly rushed off their feet, did they? They probably need the practice. You just acted on the spur of the moment, that's all. It was a mistake.'

'It is very good to have a fire drill in the middle of the night,' said Sonja comfortingly. 'If one only holds drills when it is almost breaktime, everyone knows there is no fire. This makes it more realistic. I am sure that it will not have been a wasted exercise.'

'Thank you,' said Carin. 'I hope Mr Asquith sees it that way as well. He wants to see me in his office at first break tomorrow.

He did not sound at all grateful for the opportunity of an impromptu fire drill.'

'It's that stupid snake's fault,' said Natalie. 'What a thing to keep in a school, with decent people. Uem has no right . . .'

'He was round my waist,' said Annie faintly. 'He was actually moving round my waist!' Her eyes began to glaze over.

'Come on,' said Carin. 'We'll get back to our room, we'll switch the light on and we'll all have a cup of my instant hot chocolate stuff to calm us down. You'll be fine. I just hope they manage to find Neru.'

They all sat huddled on Annie's bed with a cup of hot chocolate each. Annie started to laugh, although she could see the scene in the library whenever she closed her eyes, and still felt rather shaky.

'There was someone with Manfred,' Annie said suddenly. 'I had forgotten that. He had a woman with him. He came into the library with her, and they kissed. I've heard her voice before. I don't know who she was, but . . .'

'Nurse Guptah,' said Carin.

'Yeah! Yeah, you're right. How on earth did you know?'

Carin smiled. 'When Uem and I went past the lodge we saw the light in his little guard room or whatever it is. And we heard them talking. Well, not just talking . . .' she giggled. 'There was a bit of kissing, too. At least, I assume so. There were gaps in the conversation . . .'

'Manfred and Nurse Guptah! Well. They never show any sign of it during the day, do they? I'd never have guessed.'

'They're certainly very discreet,' said Sonja approvingly. 'But that is as it should be. It is not seemly for staff to carry on romantic affairs in front of the pupils . . .' She broke off. 'Why are you looking at me like that?' she demanded.

'You just sound so much like a headmistress,' grinned Carin.

'That is indeed what I wish to be in the future,' said Sonja calmly. 'And I will not allow such carrying on in my school, I assure you. We would all have been expelled by now, in a properly run establishment.' She smiled. 'On the other hand, in order to be the most excellent of headmistresses, and to be one step ahead of the naughty pupils, one must first develop an intimate knowledge of naughtiness. Is this not the case?'

A soft knock at the door revealed Uem, smiling broadly, and Lance. 'May we enter, and perhaps partake of whatever excellent substance is wafting that delicious aroma to my very nostrils?' asked Uem.

'Come on in,' said Annie. 'You found the creature, then?'

Uem bowed. 'Neru was most frightened by his distressing encounter with you,' he said disapprovingly.

'HE was frightened!' snapped Annie. 'Well, forgive me if I don't seem too worried about poor old Neru, mate. I'm too busy recovering from the prospect of being crushed to death.'

'Neru would not have harmed you,' said Uem. 'Not in any serious degree. But he is now taking his ease within my suit of armour, and by the time dawn breaks upon another day I am confident he will be fully reassembled.'

'Recovered,' supplied Annie. 'Which is more than can be said for me. Anyway, forget all that now. What about Manfred and Nursie, eh?'

No one felt much like sleeping, and they talked until it was almost dawn, inventing wilder and wilder stories about improbable romances between members of staff, and working out what any children of such a union would be like. Letty Domingo would fall passionately for Clingon the bursar, they decided, since opposites attract. Their child would be blessed with a wild imagination and an excellent head for figures – 'all the right ingredients for a good fraudster,' said Annie. 'Then, if you get caught, you also have the ability to write and sell a great tabloid newspaper story about your long life of crime.'

'It is high time we got to the bottom of what that man is up to,' said Carin. 'But for now, I'm going to have to plead with you all to wind down and get off to bed. I'm shattered, and I've got to think of a reasonable story for Mr Asquith tomorrow . . .'

Back in the headmaster's house, Charles and Petal were sitting up in bed drinking a soothing cup of tea and nibbling on chocolate digestive biscuits, both supplied by Charles before his wife had sufficiently recovered her wits to offer a soothing root potion.

'The girl said she was having a nightmare and sleepwalking,' said Charles. 'Can you do both at the same time, I wonder? I've never come across such a thing before. The fire glass which set off the alarm was downstairs by the kitchen. That's quite a way from the bedrooms.'

'The poor child must be deeply troubled,' said Petal in a low voice. 'So far from home, and low of spirit. And no mother or father on hand to comfort her. So her soul roams the night, searching for security, and her mind plays out the deepest fears of the dark and tortured night. You must let me help her, Charles. You must. What torment she must be in, Charles, what torment.'

'Mmm, perhaps,' said Charles sceptically. He looked at Petal, who grew more beautiful to him with every passing year. She had such a tender heart, she could not bear to think of anyone being in distress. Her eyes were filled with tears. He put his hand to her face and kissed her gently.

'Petal, my love, I am sure you can do a lot of good for this poor young girl, if indeed there is something troubling her. I will listen to what she has to say tomorrow, and if I feel she is in need of some personal support, I will send her straight to you, I promise.'

'Yes, oh yes, indeed, Charles, you must.' Petal glowed with

warmth. At last Charles was beginning to see the light. Usually she could not help feeling that her husband was deeply distrustful of her philosophies, and at times she was sure he was deliberately keeping her from reaching out to the students in this way. But tomorrow she would take the dear distressed girl under her wing and these night terrors would become a thing of the past.

Two birds with one stone, thought Charles smugly. Petal would keep herself occupied planning out a course of therapy for Carin Kemp. And Charles could picture no more fitting punishment for such an irresponsible act as this girl had indulged in tonight, than to be the sole focus of the devoted attention of Petal Butterkiss. He would make sure that she was invited to tea – that would really make her see the error of her ways, he was sure. He would encourage Petal to bake a cake for her.

A great idea suddenly struck him. Why not make Petal a sort of school counsellor? He had been impressed by the very good health record at the school since appointing Amina Guptah as school nurse. Before she came, there had been a small and steady stream of visitors to the san, usually during those lessons for which the 'invalids' had little enthusiasm. Old Nurse Smith had dished out tea, biscuits and sympathy. Nurse Guptah's approach was far better for the pupils' health. Charles was well aware that you would have to be very sick indeed before you visited Nurse Guptah. What if he took a similar approach to disruptive pupils? You could make a strong argument for bad behaviour being a symptom of a troubled mind, as Petal clearly believed. Why not refer badly behaved children to her for her own special brand of counselling? Charles was sure people would reform their behaviour rather than sample Petal's 'therapy' twice. Yes, he would certainly think that over, tomorrow. Charles snuggled down beside his wife with a smile, and turned out the lamp.

Chapter 8

*I*t was lunch-time before Carin could tell her friends about her interview with the headmaster. She looked miserable as she trailed into English etiquette. This weekly lesson was devoted to table manners, polite conversation and silverware. Uem and Sonja were completely fascinated. Annie and the others found it tedious.

'Sorry I'm late,' Carin muttered to Madame Deviska.

'Please do not worry about it, Miss Kemp,' said Madame Deviska, in an English accent so close to perfect it betrayed her foreign origins immediately. The last letter of a word was sometimes held for just a fraction of a second too long. 'The stumbling manner of your, forgive me, rather inadequate apology presents me with an excellent practical example of what not to do when one finds oneself in the unfortunate position of arriving tardily for a function, thereby placing oneself at risk of offending the hostess and causing unnecessary inconvenience to the other guests and, indeed, to the hostess.'

'Or host?' supplied Lance helpfully, in one of his rare talkative moments.

Madame Deviska clearly did not regard hospitality as having anything to do with men, and glared at Lance before continuing.

'Now listen carefully. Miss Kemp will leave the room and make her entrance again. This time, she will have her head up, like so. . .' Madame Deviska demonstrated by thrusting out her chin. 'She will have a ready smile upon her lips – not too broad, for this would denote insincerity in the apology which is to follow. However, she will of course have a good reason for arriving late . . .' she looked meaningfully at Carin, who nodded glumly, 'which she will be explaining to her hostess. Therefore, she has no need to be too apologetic. English people of culture do not apologise profusely for anything, even when they are at fault. It is a trait of common and vulgar people to be constantly apologising. Now, Miss Kemp. I would like you please to leave the room, enter again, and deliver your apology with some sense of style and grace. Off you go.'

Carin remained rooted to the spot, her face turning crimson. She felt bad enough about what she had done last night, the folly of which had been amply brought home to her by Mr Asquith. This further humiliation was too much. Annie could see the tears building up in Carin's eyes. Madame Deviska, however, was unmoved.

'We are waiting for your presentation, Miss Kemp.'

There was an agonising pause.

'Madame Deviska, may I crave your indulgit?' Uem had risen to his full height, which was considerable when you added the effect of the robes and hat.

Madame Deviska, who was a complete snob, glowed and bowed slightly. 'Your Highness?' With everyone else, Uem had insisted on being known simply by his first name. Madame Deviska, however, had been so excited at the prospect of real royalty in her class that Uem had good-naturedly played along. He always dressed in special festival clothes for her lessons, and was at his most regal. It was an impressive sight, when Uem 'put on the glitz' as Annie called it.

'Miss Kemp is covered with confusion at so great an honour as the opportunity to engage in one of your little demon stations of the finer points of English etiquette. Madame, I am a very keen student of the art and it is of course vital to my honoured father that I learn these little niceties. I wonder, with your permission, if I might demon state on Miss Kemp's behalf?'

'Demonstrate, your Highness. It is one word, you see. Well, I . . . yes, of course, if you wish. Miss Kemp, you may sit down.'

Carin scuttled to her seat and Uem swept out of the room. The whole class watched the door in anticipation. There was a long pause. Madame Deviska began to look rather uncomfortable. Still nothing happened. Just as she was about to suggest someone go into the hallway to see what the prince was doing, the door was flung open. One of the younger children who had happened to be passing on his way to a clarinet lesson walked in, carrying Uem's ornate red lacquered pencil tin. He threw petals (hastily gathered, Annie guessed, from the rose trees which grew just outside) on to the floor. He announced, in a rather confused and startled tone, 'His Royal Highness, Uem Taddy . . . gogo . . . ornn, Lord of the Islands, High Ruler of . . . I forgot that bit . . . is arriving.'

He stood to one side and gestured towards the door with a wide sweep of his arm. Uem entered, with a measured step, crushing the petals underfoot. The slight scent of roses hung in the air. He slipped the younger boy a ten-pound note, then he took Madame Deviska's hand, bowed low and kissed it.

'Madame Deviska, I do apologise for being tardy. The chauffeur had not realised the traffic would be so heavy at this time of day, being unacostumed to this area of town. I do hope I have not greatly inconvened you or my fellow gusts.'

'Not at all, I assure you,' murmured Madame Deviska.

Uem bowed low again and returned to his seat with a huge smile. Carin gave him a grateful little wave.

'Thank you, your Highness, for demonstrating to us how a person of innate breeding and culture should behave in such a circumstance. However, if you will forgive me, I might venture to suggest that in England, picking your hostess's rose petals and strewing them over her carpets might not be seen in an amicable light. It would be better, I think, to leave the rose beds unmolested. Apart from that, well done, your Highness. Well done.'

Madame Deviska remained sweet for the rest of the lesson. It would be something to tell her fellow members of the Amateur Romantic Novelist Society tonight. What a great romantic hero a character such as Prince Uem would make.

'So what happened?' demanded Annie as soon as they escaped from Madame's clutches into the dining-hall.

Carin took her can of Coke from the drinks machine and flipped the top. She drank in silence. 'Oh, I have needed that!'

'Was it that bad?' asked Sonja sympathetically.

'Worse,' said Carin. 'She told me it was made with honey and plums – so why did it taste so salty?'

'What are you on about? Come on, don't keep us in suspense.' Annie took the can away from Carin. 'What happened, Carin?'

'Well, I went into the head's room expecting a real rocket, you know, and some sort of awful punishment like extra etiquette lessons, or whatever. But he was really gentle and sweet . . . it was much worse than being angry.'

'What did he say?' asked Sonja.

'He said I had to understand that what I had done last night was a very serious thing and that it worried him greatly. We were lucky that the engines hadn't been needed elsewhere, or I could have been responsible for a terrible calamity. Then he told me some of the younger ones had woken up with bad dreams after they went back to bed. Nurse Guptah had to hold a clinic this morning . . .'

'Every cloud has a silver lining for somebody,' said Annie.

'No, it wasn't funny, Annie. I felt awful about it. I did understand what he meant. Anyway, I said I was sorry, I knew it was stupid, but I had dreamed this weird dream and suddenly found myself in the corridor . . . I just said I didn't know what had come over me and I was terribly sorry and I would never do it again. Then he said he was sure I hadn't meant it . . .'

'Sounds OK to me,' said Annie. 'In other words, he let you off with a bit of a guilt trip.'

'Not at all,' said Carin grimly. 'He said that since it seemed I hadn't actually meant to do it, there was an indication of some kind of emotional turmoil. He referred me for counselling. . . to Petal.'

'Petal? Oh, no – you poor thing.' Annie was immediately sympathetic.

'He sent me to her straight away to arrange things. She gave me a drink of that nasty tea. . .'

'Tea!' echoed Lance. His hair waved in disgust.

'But not food as well?' interrupted Uem, with a look of pure horror.

Carin nodded. 'A whole piece of cake. Well, I think it was cake. She called it soul food. She's going to assess my karmic balance and tutor me in deep breathing, stress management and expressing my deepest feelings. She thinks we will need at least four sessions together.'

'Four!' said Lance.

'At least!' added Sonja.

'And all with food!' exclaimed Uem with a grimace.

Carin's friends contemplated this possibility in awed silence for a minute. Finally, Uem said, 'It was most gracious of you to keep from telling the truth in the face of such a gruesome connie-quence. Neru and I will not forget your kindness, Carin. We are full of gratefuls. I will ensure that my father bestows upon you the appropinate honour for your service to the royal person.'

'Yeah, thanks, Uem. That'll be lovely,' said Carin politely. 'Well, at least half-term is coming up next week. Petal suggested that we start after the holiday, for continuity. So I'm counting on you lot to make sure I have a brilliant time in France, to build up my strength. I'm going to need it.'

'I wish you were coming with us,' said Natalie to Annie. 'We're such a clan now, it will be odd not having you there.'

There was a general murmur of agreement. Annie was surprised to feel a twinge of regret herself. But she knew that going home was the right thing to do. She longed to see Mum and Dad again, to tell Emma and Gayle all about this weird school, and catch up with their gossip about all her old friends.

'You lot just have a great time. Bring me back some souvenir photographs and a Mickey Mouse umbrella or something.'

The half-term week went very quickly for Annie. Her parents daily exclaimed that she seemed quite grown-up all of a sudden. She had to tell them, with as much detail as she could remember, all about the school and the lessons and her new friends. Her mother was enthralled by the tales of English culture and heritage, and the etiquette lessons. Annie showed her how to set the table for formal dinner, and Mrs Tompkin insisted that she would lay things out properly in future. She dashed off to buy a whole new set of cutlery, complete with ornate mahogany case, as they had no fish-knives.

'Imagine,' she said to Annie's father. 'Fish and chips of a Thursday night for nigh on forty years, and never using the right knife. What were we thinkin' on?'

'But we don't have to give up eating fish and chips, do we?' asked Annie's father anxiously. He regarded his new fish-knife with suspicion, and then looked mournfully down at his plate, where lay the Dover sole, potato croquettes and mixed salad his wife had prepared.

'No, no. It just didn't seem right to christen our expensive new cutlery with something as common as a fish supper from the local chippy. Back to normal next Thursday, promise.'

Annie and her father breathed a sigh of relief.

There was a slight strain between Annie and Emma and Gayle when they got back together at first, but within half an hour they were chatting away as if they had never been parted. They swam, did each other's hair, tried out new nail varnishes, went to the cinema, took a boat out on the river, and generally spent every day of the half-term break happily in each other's company.

Annie made Gayle and Emma promise that they would come with her parents to the Arthur Festival at the end of term. This annual festival marked the day King Arthur's funeral cortège supposedly passed through the village on its way to the unknown burial site of the great king, the true Avalon. There would be stalls, rides, a procession and of course the school production, 'Scenes from Camelot', for which they would be expected to rehearse almost nightly after Annie got back. For King Arthur's English Academy, it marked fittingly the last day of term, and Annie could travel back home with her family and friends for Christmas. Gayle and Emma readily agreed. They wanted to see this place for themselves.

'Sounds a complete loony bin to me,' said Gayle. 'You've given it six weeks. I think that should be enough. Bradford High may be boring, but at least you don't have chimps in school uniform and snakes slithering over you. Come back home, lady. Just leave them to it.'

It was very tempting. Annie had begun to fear that if she stayed at King Arthur's for too long, she would become crazy too. And would she know that she was crazy in time to escape? Or would she just sink slowly into it, so that she became like all the others, and people looked at her and said, 'That Annie Tompkin is a real headcase,' behind her back?

'No. I can stick it out, at least for a bit longer,' she told Gayle firmly. 'Mum and Dad are so excited about being with all those rich and famous people at the parents' do. And Carin's not weird at all. She's sensible. Natalie is only strange when she wears her PE kit – the rest of the time she's OK. And Uem and Lance are harmless weirdos. Granted, Sonja is a bit unpredictable. You never know what she's going to do next. But they are turning into good mates, you know? Not like you and Emma, but I would miss them all. We have an agreement that if one of us sees the other one going strange, we'll say so.'

'You all sound a bit loopy,' said Gayle. She gave Annie a hug. 'I think it's brill, the way you're sticking it out. But think again at Christmas. Don't stay the whole year. You'll be a fruitcake. I guarantee it.'

Annie was taken to the train station by her parents with a huge bag groaning with cake, fruit and cans of drink. Her mother had been, in childhood, an avid reader of boarding-school books. She knew that pupils at such schools needed a 'tuck hamper' at the start of each term, and that midnight feasts were a regular occurrence. She did not want Annie to miss out. Annie tried in vain to convince her that these days the food at schools like hers was really quite good, and that she hadn't been near a single midnight feast.

'That's because you're only just settlin' in,' said her mother wisely. 'You'd best be prepared, lass. You don't want to go short, or not be able contribute your fair share . . .'

Annie could hardly bear to leave her parents on the platform, knowing how much they would miss her. The funny thing was, though, that although she felt really miserable all through the journey, when she saw her room again she felt all right, and actually looked forward to meeting up with the others and hearing about the trip to EuroDisney.

'It was great during the day, at least for the first couple of days,' Natalie told her. 'We got to roam around the park and try out all the rides. But we had to be back at the hotel by five o'clock – and guess who was our group leader . . .'

'Madame Deviska,' said Uem enthusiastically. 'It was a stroke of the most good fortune. The other groups had teachers who were only interested in having a good time. They went out to the park again in the evenings, and dined upon hamburgers and other unsuitable food. But those of us who were blessed by the presence of Madame were able to take advantage of some extra tuition in table manners by dining in the hotel, in our own suite, conversing upon the topic of the day. We could hardly believe our luck . . .'

'You can say that again,' said Carin glumly. 'It was all riveting stuff, Annie, as you can no doubt imagine.'

'It was very kind of Madame to give us so much of her time,' said Sonja primly. 'None of the other teachers spent all evening with their group. Mr Leddan's pupils were told to . . .' she went red in the face, '. . . to go away and amuse themselves, although those were not his exact words. As long as they were back by midnight, he did not seem to care what they were doing. He and Miss Domingo spent almost every evening in the hotel bar.'

'Scandalous!' breathed Annie, amused.

'But then, on our last night, Madame got ill,' said Natalie.

'Something she ate,' said Carin meaningfully, looking at Lance.

'Lance, you didn't . . .' said Annie.

'Yep,' said Lance.

'It wasn't anything really awful,' said Carin. 'Some organic thing that Lance came across by accident when he was researching his woodworms. It's a plant that makes you feel seasick.'

'Unless you lie down,' said Lance. His eyes, as ever, were invisible, but his teeth flashed a wide smile from beneath his fringe.

'So we had a great time on the last night,' grinned Sonja. 'Although I personally quite enjoyed the other nights, too, I could see the merit in having a change of scene.' She sprang up from her chair and adopted the posture of Madame. Sonja was superb at capturing the voice and body movement of just about anybody. She sounded just like their teacher. 'Do forgive me, children,' she sighed. 'I feel rather unwell. I must ask you to excuse me from this evening's conversation. Please do your best without me . . .'

'It sounds a real laugh,' said Annie. 'So, what happened to Neru over the holiday, Uem? Presumably you didn't take him with you.'

'The excellent Mr Plumberry, village vet, gave Neru board and lodging for me,' said Uem. 'He is a kind and discreet gentleman, most fascimilated by reptiles. His wife will not allow him to keep one of his own, but he has offered to foster Neru whenever it is necessary.'

'Tell Annie what he told us,' said Carin.

'Ah, yes,' said Uem. 'When Carin and I went to pick up Neru, Mr Plumberry asked us whether I knew anything about the school's involvement with horse-racing,' said Uem.

'Horse-racing?' echoed Annie, mystified.

'Mmm, strange, isn't it?' said Carin. 'Remember we thought that paper Clingon had in the Blue Dolphin had something to do with horses, and we didn't know what? Listen to this.

Apparently, King Arthur's English Academy has two horses in training at a stables in the south of Ireland somewhere. Mr Plumberry's not sure where, exactly. He only knows about it because one of his old university friends is the consultant vet to the Racing Federation or something over there. They met up at a conference for vets, and that's where he heard about it.'

'Why would the school be getting involved in horse-racing?' asked Annie.

'You may well ask. Especially as it is such an expensive and risky business,' said Natalie. 'Some of the horses my father trains are owned by four or five people – it's so expensive to own a whole horse, you see. Some have shares in a couple of top runners. So to have two promising runners owned by one smallish school. . .'

'You are talking about serious money,' said Sonja. 'Now, see if you can guess the name of the man with whom the vet has to correspond if there is an urgent problem concerning the health of the horses.'

Annie said, 'It would have to be Clingon, right?'

Her friends nodded.

'Do you think the head knows? I mean, do you think it's a proper business investment on behalf of the school?' asked Annie.

'Nope,' said Lance.

'Too high-risk, I would have thought,' said Carin.

'Well, well,' said Annie. 'Our first clue. We are going to have to find out a bit more about this. Who knows what Clingon has been up to, or for how long? But we need to be careful. We have to find out what it is he's doing, where the money is coming from, and who else is in it with him.'

'How are we going to do that?' asked Natalie.

Annie frowned. 'Just at the moment, I have no idea.'

Chapter 9

Rehearsals for the 'Scenes from Camelot' pageant were held almost daily after the half-term break. Petal Butterkiss and Letty Domingo were beginning to show the signs of strain. They both had the artistic temperament, or as Annie's mother described it, 'easy to get in a lather, but nothing gets washed.' Annie could see what she meant, now that she had met this pair of luvvies.

Each rehearsal started with what Letty called 'warm-up exercises' and Petal termed 'preparing to dig'.

'You are digging deep into your souls,' she explained, looking like a witch doctor in her floaty robes. 'Dig down into the pain, the anxiety – this is where true creativity is to be found, this is where your character's motivation and your true skills as an actor are hiding, waiting for you to *claim them from the shadows...*' When she got to the bit about claiming from the shadows, Petal swept her arms upwards as if she were challenging dark and brooding skies.

She looks just like one of those warriors you see in the films, thought Annie, where they make their last great speech against the night sky, the day before going into battle. What a pity it's lunchtime and broad daylight outside – it sort of spoils the effect . . .

After the preparation to dig came the straightforward stuff – rehearsing the show. Letty had insisted that Uem rehearse his part without putting on the suit of armour; she said it was unnecessary until the dress-rehearsal at least.

'But I am truly guttered!' wailed Uem in despair. 'For it is such a noble and wonderful suit of armoury, is it not? And to wear it only for one night. It cannot seem to be just, Miss Domingo, it cannot!'

'Nonetheless,' said Letty firmly. 'It is not a good idea to risk damaging it in rehearsal. We want it to look wonderful for the real thing, don't we, Uem? Besides, how could I let you wear your costume and not let everyone else wear theirs? You do see the problem, don't you?'

'Ah but yes, of course, I am not to have special privilets because of the royal personage, Miss Domingo. My father has made that clear. He understands, as of course I do myself, that England is a democrappy . . .'

He turned with a faintly injured air as three Junior school girls giggled.

'Democracy is the word you want, Uem,' said Letty with a smile. 'But yes, I can see you're with me on this one. Thank you. Right, everybody, positions please.'

They ran through their parts, which were coming together quite nicely now that everyone had more or less learned their lines. The sad parting between Lancelot and Guinevere, played by George and Eloise in year eleven, was particularly moving. They acted really well – you could believe they were in love.

'Such talent,' breathed Petal. 'You can feel the chemistry between them. It puts me in mind of one particular scene I had in *We Die Tomorrow* . . . oh yes, look at that kiss. So tender, so loving. One could almost believe . . .'

The kiss is certainly realistic, thought Letty. They seem to have rehearsed it down to the last detail.

Usually when teenagers rehearsed love scenes they giggled for a while and had to be persuaded to take it seriously. Then there was always that awkward moment when they both turned their heads the same way, or one squealed that the other smelled of garlic, or had wet lips. But these two young people got straight down to it without any embarrassment whatsoever.

A fascinated silence fell on the hall as the other characters gathered to watch.

'Do you think it should be such a long kiss?' Letty asked hesitantly, when their lips had been locked for a full minute.

George and Eloise did not appear to hear her. Letty shuffled uncomfortably.

Petal, locked in some dream memory of her own, did not appear to be at all worried.

'For God's sake, put him down, Eloise!' came a voice. Stephanie Harvey had entered the hall.

George and Eloise parted lips, reluctantly, and looked sulkily at Stephanie.

'Haven't you two eaten today?' she asked acidly. 'This is family entertainment. I really think the village has enough rumours and gossip about what goes on here already, don't you?'

'The directors of the scene don't seem to find it offensive,' said George, whose father had made a lot of money in films. 'And you can't impose arbitrary censorship on what is, essentially, an artistic interpretation by actors hired to play a part. Lancelot and Guinevere really had the hots for each other, right? Well, our job is not to pander to the backward prejudices of the local community – our job is to act, to make those characters come alive.'

'Great speech,' murmured Petal.

'That's the trouble with giving your leading role to the offspring of a film director,' said Stephanie. 'He knows all the patter off by heart, don't you, George?'

She stepped up to the stage. 'So it's an act, is it?' she asked George. 'In the real world, you and Eloise haven't got the hots for each other, as you so delicately put it. You are not taking these two generous, gullible directors here for a ride; you would play the scene the same way whoever the partner was, is that it?'

Eloise, who was in Stephanie's form and could see the trap opening, kicked George on the shin. But poor gullible George walked straight into it. 'Of course,' he said, with great dignity.

'Well,' smiled Stephanie, 'I certainly look forward to seeing the same acting talents on display when each of you goes through the scene with an understudy. I'm sure they'll really learn a lot from the experience. Now, could we just see that scene once more, please, George and Eloise?'

George and Eloise looked at each other in dismay. Hattie Barcroft, who was Eloise's understudy and quite a fan of George's, even though he was four years above her in the school, gave him a broad, eager smile, showing the full range of the orthodontist's extensive metalwork.

George sighed, and took Eloise in his arms. The kiss was substantially shorter this time, and not half as passionate.

Petal Butterkiss looked reproachfully at Stephanie, who she saw as an over-practical person with no artistic leanings, for all that Charles seemed to think her very competent.

But Stephanie simply said, 'Well done. You don't look as though you're trying to reach each other's tonsils now. Make sure it stays that way, if you please. Now, Letty, there's a Mr Jones here about the horses for the pageant.'

'Horses!' squealed Petal excitedly. 'Real horses! But of course, the knights would not be walking through the village like common peasants. They would be mounted on the most noble of steeds . . . How clever of you, Letty, to think of horses.'

'Um, donkeys actually,' said Letty apologetically. 'We did ask the local pony club if we could borrow a few ponies to pull Arthur's funeral carriage, but they weren't too keen – bit highly strung for that sort of thing. But the donkeys – their names are Daisy and Tulip by the way – come highly recommended as trustworthy and reliable, as long as you keep feeding them.'

'Trustworthy and reliable,' repeated Petal. In her voice, the words sounded like vague insults. 'Yes, I see. When you said horses I . . . I went into a flight of fancy, forgive me. I was picturing Lancelot and Gawain side by side, in the final test of friendship and loyalty, in a torchlit glade, each on his horse, tails swishing, noble thoroughbred companions carrying their masters to the doom and grief of the burial grounds. I just cannot be sure that . . . Daisy and Tulip are quite the same thing. Well, well; one must compromise, I suppose.'

Letty went off to talk to Mr Jones about the part Daisy and Tulip were to play in the legend of King Arthur, and the rehearsal went on under Petal's direction. She noted that Annie Tompkin seemed quite distracted, and had to be reminded twice to move into her place. Also, she seemed not to be keeping up with the others during the local bustle scenes. Thank goodness she has a non-speaking part, thought Petal, with smug satisfaction. She had been right to veto Letty's suggestion that Annie would make a good actor, after all. The sense of occasion was clearly too much for the child. Even Lynchpin, with his bit part as Lady Guinevere's companion, was keeping up better than Annie, poor girl.

Annie's friends, who knew her better, couldn't figure out what the glazed look on her face was about. It remained all afternoon – you couldn't get a sensible word out of her. 'I'm thinking,' was all she would say.

At supper, she crumbled a roll into her soup without paying any attention to it. It was the same with the main course, where she ate very little, and when Uem took her dessert and ate it himself, Annie just smiled at him vaguely and nodded.

'What is the matter with you?' demanded Carin finally. 'You've had a soppy half-smile on all afternoon, and no one can get any sense out of you. Come on, it's time to put us out of our misery.'

'I think I've worked it all out,' said Annie. 'It's smart, it's audacious, it may get us all expelled but, what the hell? Who would like to do something, really DO something, about paying Clingon back for defrauding the school? Well, for defrauding us, I suppose I should say, since it's our families that fork out the money he swindles.'

'I thought we'd agreed we could do very little,' said Natalie. 'That is, if he is on the fiddle, as you put it. We don't know for sure, do we? If we go to the head or the police we don't know what to say. We have no evidence – sure, they'll not be believing a bunch of kids, will they?'

'You're right, we can't do anything officially, not yet,' said Annie. 'But there are many ways to skin a squirrel, as my old gran always says. We've got to find out more about those horses.'

'How do we do that?' asked Sonja.

'Simple,' said Annie. 'We break into Clingon's office!'

Chapter 10

*A*nnie smiled at her friends, who looked confused. 'My bet is that Clingon would keep whatever he's got under everyone's nose – in the school. So, how do we get into his office?'

'From outside,' said Lance.

'How, though?' asked Carin. 'He's unlikely to leave his window open for us.'

'They are quite old windows,' said Annie, looking at Lance. 'I expect they have those slide locks.'

Lance grinned. 'No problem.'

'Are you saying you think you can get in at the window, even if it's locked?' asked Carin.

'Sure,' said Lance.

'I hoped you'd say that. Listen, how come you're so confident at cat-burglary, anyway?' asked Annie, remembering the easy way Lance had climbed in at the window the night they went to the Blue Dolphin. 'Where on earth did you learn those little tricks?'

'Dad's chauffeur,' said Lance.

'A useful education indeed,' said Sonja. 'So Lance gets in at the window, and opens the door for us. What then? What are we looking for, exactly?'

'I'm not sure. Papers of some kind, something that will at least tell us where the horses are, and some names,' said Annie. 'Remember, Clingon knows that the headmaster can hardly add two and two. He's not going to worry about keeping all his records on school premises. He's a weasel, the type that would get some enjoyment out of carrying on whatever it is he's up to right under the headmaster's nose. I'm sure whatever records he has will be there with his official school files, meticulously labelled so he can find them at a moment's notice, or remove them if he knows someone is likely to come looking. Now, here's something interesting. The other day I heard Mrs Batty, his secretary, talking to Miss George. Mrs Batty said he insists on doing his own filing, because that's how he keeps track in his mind. She thinks it's a very clever management strategy. I think that's rubbish. I think he files stuff himself because he doesn't want her going through the files. So we get into the filing cabinet – I presume Lance could do that easily enough . . .'

Lance nodded.

'Good. OK. Let's go over the details. Lance will go in from the garden, so we need someone to keep watch out there as well as someone outside the office door – and perhaps someone at the far end of the corridor, as well. If they see anything, they need to be able to whistle or something to give a warning.'

'I will stay in the garden,' said Sonja, 'for I can be an owl.' She cupped her hands over her mouth and gave a very convincing, and quite loud, owl hoot.

'Right,' said Annie. 'You for the garden then. What about the office and the corridor?'

'I will wander the corridor,' volunteered Uem. 'I have no idea what a filing cabinet is and do not feel confident that I would know what to do inside Mr Clingon's room. Therefore I will keep the watch. If I see anyone coming I will engage the person in a very interesting conversation about the efficacy of a nightly stroller through the garden. I believe my voice will carry round the corner to give the door guard some warning.'

The others nodded. Uem could be heard from one end of a crowded dining-room to another – and he was exactly the sort of person who would wander around and stop people with weird conversations, so he wouldn't raise suspicion.

'Me for the door,' said Natalie. 'I'll be too scared inside in the dark – I'd rather be able to see what was coming. If I hear Uem's voice, I'll knock on the door and disappear.'

'OK. Sounds like we're sorted. Lance, Carin and I will do the actual search. Here's hoping we find something – and don't get caught,' said Annie.

They chose the night Manfred was on night duty. Manfred hated patrolling the school at night. It wasn't that he was scared. When he first started in the job he had half-hoped for an armed robbery, or some other exciting event. With so many wealthy, pampered children of famous people you would expect at least an attempted kidnapping now and then. Manfred had attended many karate classes to prepare himself. He was only one grade below his black belt, and could confidently take a man apart with his bare hands, if he had to. But he never got the opportunity. Morton Gipping was a dull, remote sort of place, where everyone knew everyone's business, thanks to Charles Asquith's rather unusual approach of using village nosiness as part of his security system. Criminals and kidnappers did not seem to feel it was worth the risk. The school paid for the karate lessons, so Manfred was not complaining. But there was not exactly an incentive to patrol at night checking doors and windows. If the television was good, or if Nurse Guptah was keeping him company, Manfred left quite a long gap between his rounds.

On this particular night Bayern Munich were playing Manchester United in a cup match, so Annie was confident that Manfred would be in his room. 'We get to Clingon's office just after kick-off,' she said. 'That will give us a good forty-five minutes to have a nose around.'

The grounds were quiet in the darkness, and the air was cold. Most of the pupils were over in the warm, bustling leisure complex, watching the match or one of the films put on as alternatives. The only light visible in the administration wing was the series of soft hallway lights which were left on all night; the rest of the building was deserted.

Uem took up his post in the main hallway, just beside the swing-door which led from the main school building into the admin wing. He had dressed for the part, in dark clothes and a black scarf. Annie had insisted that he take off the balaclava, saying that no one would believe he was taking an innocent stroll through the building if they saw him dressed like that. Still, when he stood back against the wall, he was almost invisible in the shadows.

Natalie, Carin and Annie waited outside Clingon's door for Lance to let them in. Annie strained her ears to listen for signs that Lance had made it through the heavy sash windows. She heard absolutely nothing, even with her ear pressed against the door. The girls jumped when Lance swung it open.

'Easy!' he said, with a big smile.

Carin and Annie entered, leaving Natalie nervously guarding the door outside. They switched on their torches, but Lance had drawn the curtains as he came through the window, and he reckoned they were thick and heavy enough to act as a blackout. So they switched the main light on.

Clingon's office, as Annie had predicted, was immaculately tidy. He had a huge desk with clearly marked 'in' and 'out' trays, a desk tidy with sharpened pencils, several fountain pens and other bits of personal stationery. The desk drawers were not locked, and only contained headed paper, envelopes, rubber bands and paper-clips. There was a safe in the wall by the door, which Lance knew he would not be able to open.

There were two filing cabinets against the wall by the window. Neither was locked.

'He really is a cool customer, isn't he?' murmured Annie.

'Either that, or there's nothing to hide and we're here for nothing,' added Carin.

The files were all clearly marked. Annie started to read the tabs on each file. 'Admissions, current; Admissions, general; Admissions, old . . . Buildings insurance . . . Catering . . . Well, he's hardly likely to have a file marked Fraud, I suppose, so what we want could be in any of these files. It wasn't such a good idea of mine after all. He could have put all sorts of stuff in any file he liked – he's the only one who needs to know where it is.'

Annie's heart sank. To examine the contents of all the files would take all night. Also, she began to realise the seriousness of what she was doing. Reading all the files would mean she was reading confidential information about other people. She hadn't thought about that. It was like prying into the lives of people who were completely innocent.

'Projects,' said Lance.

'What? Oh, Projects. Worth a go . . .' Annie opened the drawer marked P – Z. There was indeed a projects file. Inside were several large envelopes, each marked with a separate title. 'Oh look, Lance. Here's the music studio one.' Annie took out the sheaf of papers and she and Lance looked through it. There were letters between Clingon and various building and music equipment companies. He was gathering quotes for the cost of their work. A couple of letters from Lance's father in answer to queries about how much money would be available made Annie gasp. 'Is your dad really able to spend that much?'

'Sure,' said Lance with a shrug.

Annie did not say, though she couldn't help thinking it, that such a huge amount of money could be much better spent on people who really needed it. The King Arthur's English Academy was not what she thought of as a charity, exactly.

'It all looks perfectly innocent,' she said, putting the papers back. 'So what next? . . . Canteen upgrade – that'll be nice . . . Computers . . . Sauna . . . Stables. Stables, eh?' She took out the sheaf of papers. There was a letter from a Mr Ranjanshani, saying that he would like to contribute to the fund for the proposed stable block, as his daughter Jasmina had enjoyed her time at the school very much but had missed her horses. She would have appreciated the chance to stable them there. The letter was dated four years before. There were four other letters at about the same time, all responding, it seemed, to an appeal for funds to set up a stable block. The letters were all from parents whose children were no longer at the school.

'This is interesting,' said Annie. 'Clingon seems to have written to past pupils and parents, but not to anyone who might actually be around to see whether or not this stable block gets built. So maybe. . .'

There were three knocks on the door. Lance, Carin and Annie froze.

'Someone's coming!' whispered Annie. She fought down the panic that rose from her stomach into her throat. Her knees felt suddenly wobbly. Lance was already shutting the filing cabinets.

'Light!' he breathed in Annie's ear, and went over to the window. As she dashed over to turn off the light, Lance opened the curtains and pulled the window locks back into place.

While Annie and her friends had been searching Clingon's office, Uem had been strolling cheerfully along the corridor.

Alerted by the frantic owl calls from the garden, he was right by the entry door, whistling tunelessly, when the school bursar came across him.

'Good evening, Mr Clingon,' boomed Uem cheerfully.

Natalie, hearing his voice, banged on the door of Clingon's office and ran off down the corridor. There was a fire exit to the building at the other end of the hallway, but she realised as she approached that opening the door would mean breaking the seal across it and setting off the fire alarm. For a moment she froze, but then she saw the cleaners' cupboard and slipped inside to hide among the mops, dusters and disinfectant.

Clingon was very surprised to see Uem in this part of the building. He was not suspicious, however. Uem seemed completely unperturbed by being spotted in an unusual place, and was after all, thought Clingon, a prince from a land where they were given to roaming vast distances all the time. Staying in one room in a place like a school must feel quite claustrophobic.

'It is a very pleasant evening for a stroller, what, old fellow?' asked Uem. 'In my country, we spend many pleasant hours at this time of the day, when the hot sun has sunk into the horizion, visiting our friends and neighbours in surrounding villages and catching up on the goss-wipe of the day . . .'

Goss-wipe? thought Clingon. He smiled politely. 'That's very interesting, your Highness. But surely the garden would be more pleasant . . . ?'

'My thoughts exactly one hour ago,' said Uem. 'But alas! I had forgotten how very cold it is outside in this country. Never have I known such cold, Mr Clingon. Is it exceptionable for the time of year?'

'Um, no, I don't think it's an exceptional year. I do hope you will excuse me, your Highness. I must just pick up something from my office . . .'

'Oh, please do not let me detain you in any way,' said Uem pleasantly, moving smoothly into Clingon's path. 'I just miss my own people so, at this time of day in particular. You have no time for the idle chitchat with lonely pupils, of course you do not. I am so humbly apoplectic that I have intruded upon your time, Mr Clingon.'

'Not at all, I assure you,' said Clingon. As Uem had rightly guessed, he did not want to be seen as unfriendly. Uem's father was an important and wealthy man. 'I do understand how homesick you must be, particularly at this time of year when the weather is so inclement. However, my advice to you would be to embrace the difference: treat it as an adventure. The cold weather is not so bad if you consider the opportunities for winter sports, or the beauties of a frosty landscape. Perhaps you should take up photography, and become involved with the scenery around you. I am a keen amateur photographer myself, as a matter of fact. I can thoroughly recommend it as a most rewarding hobby. You could take back a beautiful pictorial record of your time with us . . .'

'What an excellent and most worthy idea!' enthused Uem – quite genuinely, for this had never occurred to him before. 'I would love to hear about this excellent pursuance in some detail. And are you a person of suitable ability to advise on the right camera and so forth, Mr Clingon?'

'Well, I . . .'

'I know my father would want me to have the best of apparatuses,' said Uem.

'Yes, of course. Let's see.' Clingon could see opportunities for himself in befriending the son of a fabulously wealthy foreign ruler. He was also quite a lonely man, and no one had ever expressed an interest in him or his hobbies before. He resigned himself to becoming entangled in one of Uem's famous drawn-out and incomprehensible conversations.

In Clingon's office, everything was back to normal. Carin, Lance and Annie were squashed together in the coat cupboard, rather inadequately hidden behind Clingon's academic gown and an old raincoat and umbrella. Annie had dived into the cupboard still carrying the envelope; it was too risky to waste time trying to put it back. She could only hope that whoever was outside wasn't Clingon, and wouldn't be looking for this particular file.

They waited in the cupboard, hardly daring to breathe, for what seemed like an eternity. Annie's first hope was dashed when they heard the door to Clingon's office open, and the light was switched on. They both stood absolutely still, squashed up together behind the flimsy garments in the cupboard, their eyes watching the cupboard door and the crack of light round it. At any moment it could spring open and Clingon would be demanding to know what they were doing in there. He would see the file, and that would be that. Annie wondered if he could be violent, or if he was perhaps working with others. What if he was just a part of an international operation of thugs and violent criminals? She shuddered.

The sound of the filing cabinet drawer being pulled open was quite distinctive. Annie closed her eyes. She thought she was going to faint; her knees began to buckle under her. Carin and Lance, on either side of her, were squashed up so tightly that it occurred to Annie that even if she fainted, she would not fall.

There was a long pause, during which Annie could not work out at all what was happening. Then the light went out, and the door closed. Still they waited, afraid to move in case he came back.

Just as they were beginning to relax the door opened again. They all froze.

'Are you still here?' It was Natalie's voice.

With a rush of relief, Annie opened the door of the cupboard and tumbled out. She gave Natalie a fierce hug. 'I nearly had a heart attack!' she said. 'I'm definitely not cut out for a life of crime, I can tell you. Let's scarper, before something else happens.'

Uem was still in the corridor, clutching a sheaf of papers. He beamed when he saw them, and brandished the papers at them. 'The excellent Mr Clingon has given me much valuable information about an excellent new hobby,' he said. 'I will take up the photography as from to-very-morrow. I will document and catalogue the misery and the pleasure of an English winter, and this will mamuse and delight my people upon my return.'

'Well done for keeping him talking,' said Natalie. 'I wonder why he suddenly needed to get into his office?'

'He had left behind his portable computer on his desk,' said Uem. 'He told me he was doing some paperwork at his home, and he needed it.'

'But he was definitely going through the filing cabinet . . .' said Annie. She looked at the papers Clingon had given Uem. 'Photography leaflets! Uem, I was having a heart attack in there, waiting for Clingon to discover his file was missing. And all the time you were out here, enticing him to get you something from the very same filing cabinet. He went into the cabinet to get stuff for you!'

'Just so,' beamed Uem. 'And it will change my life, I assure you. Prince Uem Taddugorrono, Photographer Extraordinary . . . I shall be a royal photographer, like your English lord who takes the pictures as well as being a royal personage for his living.'

'Mmm,' said Annie doubtfully. 'Looks like Clingon has set off yet another of your little enthusiasms, Uem. I wonder how long this one will last, eh? You must be running out of hours in the day to keep up with all the things you're already doing.'

'I am guttered at your disinterest,' said Uem. 'But no matter. I shall not be reversed in my enthusiasm for the arts.'

'Can we get out of here?' asked Natalie nervously. 'I mean, you're still clutching a file that belongs to Clingon, and he could come back at any time.'

They gathered in Uem's room, with Neru safely sleeping inside Uem's armour, and spread the papers out on the table.

'I was right,' said Annie. 'Look at all these letters – all from past pupils or parents of past pupils, all seeming to have been given information about a new stable-block that's going to be built and all arranging the transfer of money to a special account. He's on to a winner, isn't he? They're all abroad, with no direct connection to the school any more and all very busy, I expect. Why would they check that the money had been used in the way they expected? They have no reason to suppose that a place like King Arthur's would be on the fiddle. And if they should happen to visit, he can tell them the money hasn't all been raised yet. They're not to know how many people have given, or how much each person gives. He's on to a real winner. So he's taken all this money – and more, for all we know – and sunk it into what?'

'Oh, wow!' said Lance suddenly. He had been quietly reading a section of the papers from the envelope which had been clipped together.

'What is it?' asked Carin.

'Look!' said Lance.

They gathered round Lance and read the papers. There were bills of sale for two horses from a stable in Galway, Ireland: Bay Lad and Rosy Dawn.

The horses were sold to an agent, Patrick McKilroy, on behalf of a buyer in England – Clingon. There were several letters arranging stabling at an approved trainer's establishment, also in Ireland.

Natalie gasped. 'I know this place,' she said. 'My father has dealings with them. They're very well-known. We used to go to parties there, when a horse had won. My dad was best man at the wedding of Emerson, the owner of the place. Well, well. What a small world, eh?'

'So, Clingon is getting money out of people by claiming to build stables and provide horses, grooms and so on here at the school. Then he's spending the money on these two horses in Ireland. What are these, Nat? They look like the stuff Lance saw in the Blue Dolphin.'

Annie handed Natalie some charts full of figures and words which, to Annie, had no meaning. Natalie scrutinised them carefully. It took some time, and her friends stood impatiently waiting.

'He certainly had a good eye for a horse,' she said finally. 'These are form sheets – they tell you how a horse is doing, which races he's done well in, what the ground conditions were like at the time, where he originally came from, all that sort of thing. These horses are doing very well. He can't be making any money off them at the moment, but for sure they'll do well in time, so they will. It's always a risky investment, a horse, and you have to be very lucky as well as very skilful to get a winner. Our Clingon seems to have an eye – he has two potential winners here. We're talking big money, in a year or two. I'd love to know how he got hold of them. They must have cost a fortune.'

'But can we prove it's fraudulent money?' asked Carin. 'I mean, it seems to me that we have evidence Clingon is asking for money to build a new stable block for the school. We also have evidence that he has invested in two racehorses, and the bank drafts are coming from the school account. But Mr Clingon is given a free hand with the school investments, because the headmaster is such a dunce. If, as Natalie says, he has a good eye for a horse, why shouldn't he invest money in racing? All he has to do, if he's challenged, is say that he was investing in what he thought would be a good return for the school. If these horses haven't made any money yet, there is no evidence that he's pocketing the profits, is there?'

'No,' agreed Annie. 'No really strong evidence. But the money was given to build stables. He was given enough to build a school stable block, provide horses and equipment and grooms – how would he explain diverting the money to something else?'

'I do not underestimate Clingon's ability. If he is clever enough to come up with this scheme, he can surely present a plausible story for this,' said Sonja. 'We do not have in this file, as far as I can see, any cast-iron evidence for fraud. Perhaps the police will investigate and find more – but will they take it further? Are they really likely to take a story like that, coming from a bunch of kids, seriously? It is the head we should be talking to, I think. He should look at the files, and ask Clingon what's going on.'

'The headmaster is a lovely man,' said Annie. 'But he's no match for Clingon. No, we need to stop him ourselves. We need to somehow bring out what's going on in a way that will make it impossible for Clingon to keep all this a secret and start to pocket any profits these horses make . . .' She lapsed into silence, her brain working furiously.

Uem looked at his watch. 'I think we should talk again in the morning,' he said. 'I do not wish to be rude, but I have to spend some time learning my lines for the rehearsal tomorrow. I am so honoured to be Gawain the noble English knight, and I am determined not to let my fellow actors in the pageant down by not knowing my part.'

'Oh, hang on,' said Annie. 'I think . . . yes, I think I have an idea. Uem, you're a genius. Now listen up, I've got the germ of an idea here, but I need all of you to help. Petal dearly wants to have a decent pair of horses for her pageant, right?'

Her friends nodded. Carin, who was quick on the uptake, was already beginning to shake her head in disbelief.

'Right. Now, Natalie, your old man's well-known in the racing world, isn't he?'

Natalie, mystified, nodded.

'So if Clingon were to telephone a stable and say that Frank de Suza, the famous trainer, had taken an interest in the two horses Clingon has there, and had agreed to have a look at them, what do you think the response would be?'

'Depends on the stable,' said Natalie. 'If it's not well-known in its own right, it would welcome the interest. What my father does tends to get publicity in the racing world. So the stable would probably like the idea of being seen working with him. But, Annie, how . . . ?'

'Don't interrupt me, Natalie, my brain is still in full flow. Now let me just summarise what we have here. We have a problem, a possible solution, and a crop of assets which will help us make a possible solution a definite solution, with a bit of luck, of course, which every problem-solver needs.'

'You have entirely lost me in the forest,' said Uem. 'You must please to explain more simply what it is you mean. Speak it in words of one syllabub, then we may perhaps swim in your drift, as you English say.'

'OK, Uem, I get what you mean – I think!' grinned Annie. 'Now, listen: Petal wants two nice-looking horses, but Letty can only come up with a couple of flower-power donkeys. Technically, the school owns two nice-looking horses, but we don't know where they are. Possible solution: find the two horses and bring them to the school in time for the pageant. Can't you just picture Clingon's face when we present them to Petal and tell her they're actually the property of the school and so she has every right to use them in her grand spectacle?'

'You can't be serious!' said Sonja.

'She is, all right,' said Carin. 'Look at her face. We all know what that special little grin means. It's amazingly daring and creative and all that, Annie, but how on earth are you going to get it to work?'

Chapter 11

On the day of the pageant, they awoke to a heavy frost in crisp, clear sunlight. The air was cold, but with little wind. It was a good day for the celebrations. Lessons finished at eleven o'clock, to give everyone the chance to visit the street fair in the village. Annie and the others, however, met up in the school canteen as planned.

'This country is so strange,' said Uem mournfully. 'How can there be so much sun and no warmth?' He cupped his hands around his cup of hot chocolate and let the steam bathe his face.

He was wrapped up to his chin in a thick fur coat, which went down to his ankles. He had refused to listen to Carin's protests about wearing furs. He had simply said, 'If the small furry animals used in this garment had been asked, they would gladly have surrendered their lives to be of service to their prince.'

Now he drew his coat firmly round him. 'And why,' Uem groaned, 'do the English have to make these festivies outside in the cold? Me, I would place such unsocial activities well indoors, with perhaps an ebnormous wood fire burning in the grate, and an ox or two on the roasted spittle.'

'Ugh! Uem, I think you mean spit-roast. Spittle is what you spit . . .' Carin sighed at Uem's puzzled look. 'Never mind.'

Uem continued his speech unabashed. 'If this King Arthur was a sensible man, a tribal lord such as we have in my country, he would have had the good sense to travel to a warm place. There could people forever honour his memory with good food, good music, bright clothes and happy faces. Big smiling ones, not like the grim English expression so wonderfully demon-started by our good friend Natalie.'

Natalie slammed down her spoon into her coffee; there was a shower of brown liquid over the crisp white cloth. 'When are you going to get it through your thick royal skull that I am not English! Ireland is a different country, Uem. Completely different. I speak English. I am Irish. And if you don't like the weather here, why stay? If you can't hack it, go back home.'

'Hey,' said Lance gently.

There was an uncomfortable silence. Natalie was breathing heavily, close to tears.

'Natalie, I am dessicated at causing offence to you. I did not mean to slur your . . .' Uem saw the angry flash in Natalie's dark eyes, 'your neighbours' country,' he quickly added. 'You know that I am very happy here and I think English, Irish, Welsh and Scottish countries are all totally delightful. Especially Ireland, which is a land so green and pleasant to the eye. I think this, even although I have never been to Ireland and only ever saw it in pitchers. Natalie, I crave your forgivenesses. I am cold, and therefore out of good temper. This is not a thing I have known before. I do not like this weather, but I know it is a small price for staying in a country so beautiful with friends so good. Therefore, if I have caused you to be upset I am most sincerely guttered, Natalie, I promise you.'

Natalie attempted a smile. 'You have an amazing ability to grovel, Uem. I've never seen the like. It's guttered you are, is it? Look, I'm sorry, Uem. Sorry, everyone. It's just . . . well, my dad isn't coming tonight. I don't think the Ice Maiden fancies an evening at the school entertainment. Some chauffeur is coming to pick me up tomorrow to drive me to the airport. Loving family, eh?'

Annie put her arm round her friend's shoulder. She knew

that Natalie had written to Dublin last week; she had seen the letter lying ready for the post. Maybe Natalie had been hoping for a reply before the end of term. As far as Annie knew, Natalie had no contact with anyone living in Dublin, except her mother. She knew that Natalie's father had booked a hotel in Switzerland for the Christmas holiday. He and the Ice Maiden would be with Natalie for less than a week over the Christmas holiday, then they were going off to South Africa while Natalie remained in Switzerland, under the eye of a family friend. Not the best of Christmases, thought Annie. She had invited Natalie home with her, but Natalie had said she was hoping to make other plans. Were these other plans connected with that letter to Ireland? If so, Annie had a feeling Natalie's mother had let her down again.

'Let's start the day again, shall we?' said Sonja sensibly. 'We are all a little bit tense, I think. Now, when will the horses arrive?'

'They took the ferry yesterday, to make sure they had plenty of time to feed and exercise the horses properly,' said Natalie. 'They should be with Mr Plumberry by lunch-time. Sonja and I are picking them up at three, and the stable lads are coming with us in case of any problems.'

'Great. We don't want to cut it too fine,' said Annie. 'They're lighting the torches at four. The procession starts at quarter past. Now Uem, you are sure you will be able to ride this horse, aren't you?'

Uem drew up his chin. 'I am Lord of all the Islands,' he intoned, with a regal stare. 'We may not have rain and snow in such abundance as you in my country,' he said haughtily, 'but we have plenty of horses.'

'These are thoroughbred racehorses,' said Natalie quietly. 'If you're not a confident rider they'll throw you and run. They might do themselves damage.'

'And Uem, too,' added Carin.

'Well, yes, and Uem,' said Natalie, in a tone which suggested this was a pure aside to the main problem.

'Everyone got their costumes and stuff ready?' asked Annie. They all nodded.

Annie pulled the notes from her pocket and went through the list of things to do. There was an air of nervous excitement as each person confirmed where they would be and what they would do, and at what time.

'I think we've covered everything,' said Annie finally. 'There's always a huge slice of luck with this kind of thing, so fingers crossed. OK, we'd better get off to the final rehearsals.'

Letty and Petal were flitting around the rehearsal studio like a couple of demented butterflies. Annie was surprised at how nervous Petal was – she surely didn't consider this little pageant anything to worry about after years as a Hollywood star. But Petal knew only too well that studio-based films, which could be cut and edited if you did something wrong, were nothing like as risky as live performance. She wanted to do it all perfectly, to be a credit to Charles who had given her free rein with the organisation of the pageant and who had listened and supported her so wonderfully when things were getting frantic.

'Gather round, everyone,' she called. 'Into a big circle. Yes, that's it. Now, we are preparing for a major performance, so let us gather ourselves. Deep, calming breaths . . . come on now, we must breathe together, as one living organism. In, two, three . . . out, two, three . . .' There were a couple of nervous giggles at first, but soon everyone was breathing deeply in unison. Annie was surprised at how calming it was. She really did begin to feel as if she were a part of a huge, well-oiled machine, running smooth and steady.

'And stretch . . .' exhorted Petal, lifting her face to the ceiling and stretching her arms up high.

They all followed suit.

'And bend,' Petal intoned. Like saplings in a strong wind, the assembled troupe of actors and dancers followed Petal's movements, warming up for the big performance. There followed voice exercises – chants, scales, shouts and whispers, and one final 'group tuning' which involved holding hands in a big circle and trying to hear the breathing of the person next to you and mirror it in your own. Annie found this very difficult, and ended up holding her breath a lot of the time, and getting very red in the face.

As they all moved off towards the changing rooms to get their costumes on, Natalie and Sonja slipped away. The costumes they were planning to wear, which were not quite the ones Letty Domingo had provided, were in their bags. They would be put on at the stables.

Uem wanted to get into his suit of armour straight away. Petal tried to point out that this would not be a good idea, and it would be better to wait a little while longer.

'It will be very difficult to visit the bathroom in a full suit of armour . . .' she whispered tactfully.

'Please do not concern yourself,' boomed Uem. 'I have already showered this morning, and see no need to repeat such oblutions before the performance.'

Petal sighed, and gave up.

'She means when you go to the loo,' said Carin helpfully.

'And it might be difficult, in that thing,' said Annie, indicating the suit of armour which Uem had brought down to the hall in readiness.

'Not at all, I assure you,' said Uem. 'I have indeed practised many things in my armour. But if you feel it would be, as you English say, over and away to the top to don my costume now, I will indeed rephrase.'

Annie made her way to the changing room where she donned her simple peasant costume over the long johns and T-shirt vest laid out for her. Petal had insisted that each of them must have thermal underwear, so that they would not catch cold (and also, though she had not liked to say it aloud, so they would not be shivering in the cold December air and spoil the effect of her tableaux scenes). A local company had agreed to supply all the thermal underwear in return for publicity. Consequently, everyone watching the pageant would know exactly what the performers would be wearing underneath their costumes. There had already been several jokes and catcalls when King Arthur's pupils visited the village after the local newspaper story and photographs.

'Right,' said Annie. 'It's just about three o'clock. Here goes!'

At about that time, Sonja was ringing the bell at the headmaster's house, dressed as a groom. Her face was half hidden under an enormous cap into which she had bundled her hair. This, plus a woolly scarf wrapped around her throat and half over her mouth, and a few strategically placed smears of dirt, made a good disguise. Petal did not know Sonja well, so hopefully she would not recognise her at all.

Charles was out, as Sonja knew because she had telephoned him pretending to be Nurse Guptah and asking him to come over to the san urgently. Mrs Blane, the school housekeeper, answered the door. She looked suspiciously at the young lad standing on her doorstep.

'Delivery for Miss Petal Butterkiss,' said Sonja, in a strong Irish accent tutored by Natalie.

'What delivery?' asked Mrs Blane. 'If you're selling door-to-door, we're not interested, young man.'

'Sure it's horses I'm bringin',' said Sonja indignantly, waving a couple of papers in the air.

'Horses?' Mrs Blane looked out into the yard. When she saw the two sleek thoroughbreds standing quietly by the hedge, their breath misty on the cold air, her mouth fell open. Mrs Blane was not a keen follower of the horses, but even she knew a classy animal when she saw one.

'What on earth . . . ?' she stuttered.

'Would you kindly let Miss Butterkiss know that her animals have arrived. They need a bit of attention, so they do, before the pageant begins.'

'Pageant? These horses are for the pageant? Oh, my word, she's gone too far this time . . . just wait there a moment.' Mrs Blane closed the door, but not before they had heard her shrieking for Mrs Asquith in a voice edged with panic.

Petal came out into the yard swathed in a huge woollen poncho and broad hat. She looked as mystified as Mrs Blane. She stared at the horses, at the stable lads astride them, and at the young person in a heavy jacket and riding cap standing between them, who she thought might be a girl, but it was difficult to tell as the person didn't look up at her. Then she turned her beautiful and mystified eyes upon Sonja, who to her eyes was another stable lad.

'I . . . excuse me, I think there must be some kind of misunderstanding here. We are expecting two donkeys from the village . . . These are not donkeys, are they?'

Sonja sniffed in disgust at this insult to 'her' animals. 'If it were donkeys you were after, sure you'd have been better off asking the gypsies, not a proper established stable,' said Sonja. 'Will you not be wantin' them then, Miss?'

'I . . . they're wonderful, just wonderful. But I don't know where they've come from. It's all very confusing.'

Sonja snapped her papers officiously, and read, 'Two thoroughbreds for the Arthur pageant. Deliver to care of Miss

Petal Butterkiss, Headmaster's House, King Arthur's English Academy. No message.'

Suddenly Petal remembered Charles's gentle smile at breakfast that morning, when she had been nervously checking and rechecking her list of things to do. 'It will all be lovely, Petal,' he had said. 'You deserve every success, and I wish I could think of a way to help.'

This must be Charles's way of helping. She had indeed commented that Gawain and Lancelot would look a bit dismal walking, when in reality they would have had valuable horses, but she had not realised Charles was listening and taking notice.

Petal's eyes filled with tears. 'The wonderful, wonderful man . . .' she breathed. 'They're from Charles Asquith, aren't they?'

Sonja sniffed again and consulted her papers. 'It says nothing about who they're from,' she said. 'I've brought them from Greenacre Stables for a Miss Butterkiss, that's all I know. Now, do you want them or not?'

'Yes, yes, of course I want them. Thank you so much. I . . . wait there, I'll escort you over to the pageant assembly point. I was just about to leave myself.' Petal rushed off to get her scripts and basket of props.

'So far so good,' breathed Sonja to Natalie. They grinned at the stable lads, who had viewed Petal with some awe. They had been told not to speak unless they absolutely had to, and they were sticking to their word. They had no idea what was going on, only that the horses were going to be involved in the pageant. They had both been very worried at first – this was not something they felt racehorses ought to be involved in – but they had been won over by Natalie's calm and quiet confidence with the horses, and of course with her father's reputation. She had convinced them that this was a crucial part of good training. It gave the horses experience of travelling and of unexpected sights and noises, 'A bit like police horse training,' she had told them. 'It builds stamina and also helps them develop a calm temperament. I'm surprised you don't already do it – all the bigger stables do, these days. There's so much going on at racetracks these days, eh? Bomb scare or an animal rights protest sort of thing, they are happening all the time. But these horses won't go to pieces, because it won't be strange to them, will it? They're prepared for the worst. My father does this all the time . . .'

Back at the pageant assembly point, Letty was assembling the players into their positions ready for the procession.

'We only have fourteen peasants,' she said. 'Where are the other two? Not down with flu or something, I hope?'

'Just gone to the loo, Miss Domingo,' said Annie cheerfully. 'They'll be back in a minute. Don't worry, they know exactly where to stand.'

'Right. Where is Gawain? Uem, where are you?'

'I am in attendance, Miss Domingo,' boomed Uem from behind her. His armour rattled slightly.

'Right. Oh I say, Uem, you do look wonderful. That headpiece positively gleams in the torchlight. No one would know it was you under there . . . OK, off you go into the line. Lancelot? You go behind him. Now . . .' She surveyed the docile donkeys bearing Arthur's funeral cart with ill-disguised disappointment. 'Could we please remember that no one is to call Daisy and Tulip by their real names during this performance, and also have we got enough carrots to keep them going if they get unco-operative?'

One of the peasants standing by the carriage nodded and patted his jacket pocket.

Letty looked at her watch. 'Three minutes to countdown –

I wonder where Mrs Asquith can be . . .'

Right on cue, Petal arrived. 'Letty, look. Do look what Charles has sent for us.' With a dramatic gesture, Petal swung her arm to indicate the horses. Bay Lad did not like the swing of the bright poncho in the torchlight. He snorted and shuffled his hooves nervously. The stable lad stroked his neck and murmured softly. Natalie held his bridle and soothed him.

'Oh my word – are they for Lancelot and Gawain? Oh, Petal, they're wonderful!' squealed Letty. 'What a kind and generous gesture.'

Letty knew nothing at all about horses. She had no idea that they were anything other than a couple of hacks from the local stable. But there was one person there who knew a thoroughbred when he saw one. Especially a thoroughbred whose training and upkeep he had diverted school funds to pay for. Charles, who arrived at that moment, had brought the school bursar with him to see the procession off. Clingon looked at the horses standing in the lane surrounded by costumed pupils, blinked, and looked again. Surely it couldn't be . . .

'Petal, where on earth did these animals come from?' asked Charles, mystified.

Petal gave him a coy smile. 'Oh, Charles, I have no idea. They appear to be a sort of anonymous love gift – and they're a wonderful surprise.' She flung her arms around her husband. The poncho waved again; Bay Lad took a few steps backwards, his ears back and nostrils flaring. 'Oh, Bunny Beaver, don't play games. I know it was you. Thank you, thank you, thank you. . .'

She started smothering her husband's face with kisses, much to the amusement of the assembled crowd. There were murmurs of 'Ooh, Bunny Beaver!' and kissing noises. Charles, embarrassed, gently pulled Petal away.

'These horses are nothing to do with me,' he said. 'Petal,

where on earth did you get them?'

'Not from you?' Petal was mystified. 'They just arrived at the house, for me . . .'

Clingon walked up to the two horses. He couldn't believe his eyes.

'Oh, good day, Mr Clingon,' said Rosy Dawn's rider, relieved at recognising the horses' owner. 'I didn't realise you would be here in person, sir. We were a bit worried to tell you the truth, that you didn't visit us in person to finalise arrangements. But as you can see, the horses are in fine form, ready for their stimulus training.'

'What the . . . I . . . stimulus training . . . ?' Clingon found himself completely unable to speak, and could only splutter in a nonsensical fashion.

'Clingon, what is all this about?' demanded Charles.

Clingon stared at the headmaster, stupefied. 'I . . . I . . .'

'I know,' said Annie, stepping out from the crowd of peasants. 'It's all a bit overwhelming, isn't it? Here, in the torchlight, you can so easily picture the scene all those hundreds of years ago. It's almost as if King Arthur himself was here watching. It was so generous of Mr Clingon to bring his own fine racehorses here for our humble procession. Not many people would risk it, but for Mr Clingon, King Arthur's always comes first.'

'Do you mean these horses are yours, Clingon?' demanded the headmaster.

'I . . . well, in a manner of speaking. I don't know, exactly . . .' Clingon's white face shone in the torchlight; his mouth opened and closed, but there was no sound.

'Shall I tell them, Mr Clingon?' said Annie sweetly.

'Shall you tell them . . . ?' echoed Clingon faintly.

'You see, sir, Mr Clingon's rich old granny died a year or so back,' said Annie. 'She left him some money – quite a bit of money, in fact. At first, he was going to make a gift to the school – this is his only home, we're all just like family to him, you see. But frankly, the school is not exactly short of a bob or two, is it? Then he was put in the way of these two very promising racehorses, and he came up with the brilliant idea of investing in them. Such interesting publicity for the school, you see? He had always intended to give them to the school when they started to earn prize money, hadn't you, Mr Clingon . . . ?'

Clingon nodded feebly.

'But when Petal said she needed horses, well . . .'

'Cor!' said one of the newsmen. 'This'll make the front page, this will. "School Bursar Gives Hollywood Star a Money-making Gift" . . .'

'Nah,' said another. 'You can do better than that. "Bursar's Bonus Saves Butterkiss Bonanza". Are you going to give him a kiss, Petal? Just one for the camera, eh?'

'Not bad. What about . . . "Millionaire's Mysterious Gift to Local School" . . . ?' said a third.

'What millionaire?' asked Charles. 'Are you a millionaire, Clingon?'

'I . . . I don't think so,' said Clingon.

'That don't matter,' said the newsman.

'I don't understand this at all,' said Charles.

'Nor me,' said Clingon. He looked as though he had arrived suddenly on another planet. He understood nothing of what was going on. His knees turned to water, and he slowly sank to the ground.

'Oh, bless him, he's so emotional about it,' said Annie serenely. 'You go on with the pageant, Mr Asquith. I'll look after Mr Clingon.'

'Are you sure? He doesn't look at all well,' said Charles

doubtfully, watching Clingon crawl into the hedgerow.

'Absolutely. He's . . . he's a very private sort of man. All this fuss and acclamation is a bit overwhelming.'

'Poor Clingon,' said Charles. 'I never guessed this was more than a job to him . . . well, well. We shall certainly be honoured to be a proper family to him from now on, you can be sure. You will look after him, won't you . . . ? Only, I think Petal will need me . . .'

'Sure. Go on, you go. I'll see to Mr Clingon.'

Charles turned to the gathered pupils, who were watching the proceedings with great interest. 'Come now, everyone. Three cheers for Mr Clingon. Hip, hip . . .'

There was a straggled chorus of cheers from the confused peasants. Bay Lad did not like this at all. He wanted his home stable and some comfortable warm hay. He showed his displeasure by bucking slightly. The stable lad reined him in and spoke to him. He hoped this stimulus training lark was tried and tested. Still, the owner would take responsibility if something happened to the horses. Jim was just doing as he was told.

'And all the time you were telling me the pageant was a waste of money and we should be content with a show in the school hall,' said Letty. 'I've got to hand it to you, Mr Clingon. You certainly know how to cook up a complete surprise.'

It did not seem to worry Letty at all that she was basically speaking to the bursar's bottom: he was still crawling away, and was halfway into the hedge. Letty beamed joyously.

'He's a very emotional sort of man, isn't he?' said Annie cheerfully. 'No wonder he didn't want anyone to know what he was planning. He probably wouldn't have been able to take the tension of all the build-up to the big day itself. Leave him alone for a while, to recover, and get on with the pageant, eh? These

155

thermal knickers are all very well, but they itch a bit. And I doubt our audience have them; they'll freeze to the spot soon.'

'Ah, yes, quite. Well, good luck, everybody,' said Charles, recovering his composure. 'You all look absolutely splendid.'

'I have a little surprise of my own,' declared Petal grandly, 'although it has been wonderfully overshadowed by Mr Clingon's astonishing gift. I gave up treading the boards many years ago, and have never regretted it. But tonight I am making a public appearance in honour of the occasion. The King Arthur Pageant, "Scenes from Camelot", will be featuring a cameo performance from myself, Petal Butterkiss, as Brusen, the evil hag.'

Petal approached the large coffin-sized wicker hamper which lay under the cloth on Arthur's funeral carriage.

'What do you doing?' asked Uem, suddenly and inexplicably nervous.

'My costume is in here,' said Petal. 'It seemed the ideal place to hide it.'

'Costume? But no, this cannot be . . . there is only a bundle of rags in there, Mrs Asquith. No costume, I ensure you.'

'Come now, Uem. What would an evil hag wear, but a bundle of rags? The Morton Gipping King Arthur Society and I have sewn it with our own hands. It is an authentic replica of an ancient witch garment. You will see for yourself . . .' Her hands were upon the hamper, her fingers fumbling with the clasps.

'Do not open the casket . . . please do not. DON'T!' wailed Uem.

Too late. Petal swung open the lid of the hamper with a flourish. She reached out her hands to gather the costume . . . and screamed.

People waiting down the lane heard it and shivered with excitement. The pageant had begun.

Neru, who had been unceremoniously evicted from the suit

of armour when Uem had realised he'd forgotten to move him in his excitement, objected very strongly to being disturbed again. He had settled down on the rags amicably enough, but now it was time to show he was not to be messed about. He raised his head, and stretched up into the air, hissing slightly.

There was an immediate commotion. Petal fainted into Letty's arms. Manfred lunged towards the carriage in an attempt to close the hamper. Uem threw down his helmet and shouted, 'Neru!' Clingon stopped in mid-sob, turned and sat in the hedge, staring at the snake in astonishment. Charles put his hand over his eyes. The little knot of reporters, who had been tipped off that the famous film star was going to announce a comeback, were delighted with yet another twist to the story of the little local pageant. Flash bulbs popped and the lane was lit up almost as if by lightning.

That was it for Bay Lad. He reared upwards, attempting to throw Jim off. When this was unsuccessful, he bucked again, sending peasants scattering for safety, and galloped off down the lane at full speed. Jim hung on, struggling for control. Rosy Dawn took off after her stable companion, and several peasants ran after the horses, squealing in a mixture of shock and excitement.

To the gathered community, standing expectantly at the roadside with their torches flaming, it was an impressive sight. Two horses suddenly came from nowhere and chased down towards the unknown burial destination, followed by a motley crew of peasants, some walking, some running, and some looking decidedly anxious. Lancelot and Gawain clanked down the lane on foot in their armour, or what was left of it. Lancelot looked totally bemused, and Gawain's distress was obvious.

After a long pause, King Arthur's funeral carriage came into view, moving at a steady pace, harnessed to two small donkeys, who wanted to see what was going on but didn't want to over-exert themselves or show too willing, since they knew that would mean fewer carrots.

'Ah, you can always tell the touch of the professional,' murmured Miss Jones-Smythe to her fellow members of the Morton Gipping Amateur Dramatics. 'I can see the hand of Petal Butterkiss in all this. Who else would think to show the knights and peasants, beside themselves with grief at the death of their king and behaving like wild creatures, contrasted with the slow and sombre dignity of the king, even in death. It's just wonderful; truly magnificent.'

This interpretation of what they were seeing quickly spread among the audience. 'Funny, that,' said Fred Bowers, a local farmer. 'Here was me thinkin' they'd made a right cock-up, and all the time it was planned. Well I never.'

No one thought to question Miss Jones-Smythe's interpretation. She knew what she was talking about, being a leading light in the amateur dramatics herself. She had once played third waitress in a real film.

Back at the start of the pageant, Annie was just crawling into the hedgerow after the school bursar. 'Is it over yet?' he asked. Clingon was hiding in the middle of the hedge. He still looked a bit shellshocked.

Annie said, 'Depends what you mean by over. You've been found out, if that's what you mean.'

Clingon shrugged. 'Win some, lose some,' he muttered. 'How on earth . . . ? Well, it doesn't matter, I suppose, how you found out.'

He crawled out of the bush and sat on the grass. He physically shook himself, shedding like a coat the pathetic air of a doomed man hiding in a bush. He looked at Annie with an entirely different expression – almost satisfaction, she thought angrily.

'You know, I've had a damn good time, considering,' Clingon said suddenly. 'Actually, I'm not very good at being a criminal. Deception is hard when people sort of instinctively feel you can't be trusted. I've never fitted in, you know. When I was small, the big children took my sweets. When I was bigger, I tried to defend myself. But they were bigger too, of course. They took my sweets *and* my bike . . . whatever they wanted.' Clingon's tone was bitter as he recalled that childhood playground.

Annie looked sceptical. Was he telling the truth, or spinning a line to make her feel sorry for him? 'Why didn't you tell your mum and dad?' she asked. 'Couldn't they have sorted out the big kids for you?'

Clingon smiled grimly. 'My father was a lawyer. He offered to sue the other children on my behalf. He wasn't even going to charge me the full fee . . .'

'Your own father offering his services for a discount? I don't believe it!' said Annie scornfully.

'Yes, it was rather good of him, wasn't it? My mother helped me a lot, too . . .'

'That's something, at least,' said Annie.

'Yes. She compiled a list of all the things that had been taken from me. Each time something happened, she would calculate the cost and add it to the list, so that when we sued, we would know what to claim in compensation.'

'So what happened? Did you get your day in court?'

Clingon shook his head. 'In the end, I couldn't afford to go ahead. I saved my pocket money for three years, but alas . . . still, it did give me an interest in accountancy, which stood me in good stead. And now – well, I bet there are opportunities for accountancy, even in prison. After all, bank robbers need financial advice as much as any businessman, don't they?'

Clingon actually began to look quite cheerful.

'You make it sound like some sort of game,' said Annie. 'Whatever happened when you were a kid, there's no excuse. What you did was dishonest – criminal. Don't you understand? You could go to prison for a long time.'

'Possibly,' said Clingon. 'On the other hand, taking into account my tragic childhood and my unblemished past . . . throw in a personality disorder if I can come up with one . . .'

'I don't think that will be a problem,' said Annie.

'There you are, then. I can line up clients while I do my porridge, or whatever the hip guys call it, and get myself a nice little business set up for when I come out. Charlton Clingon, Chief Accountant to the Criminal Classes.'

There was a proud gleam in Clingon's eye as he said this which made him look quite unhinged in the dim light. This is either a sick joke, thought Annie, or he is mad as a hatter.

'Why are you telling me all this?' she said. 'Don't you think I'm going to tell the police everything you're telling me now?'

'You're a child,' said Clingon. 'I'll just say you got over-excited about the whole thing, and no one will take much notice of what you're saying.' He laughed.

'You are a nutter,' said Annie angrily.

'And you, my dear, are a student at King Arthur's English Academy. Ever heard the one about the pot calling the kettle black?'

Annie, speechless for once, looked down the lane. A police car was edging its way up the narrow lane, blue light whirling. Someone must have called them when the horses bolted. 'There you are,' she said. 'Police car. Are you going to tell them about this, or shall I?'

Clingon scrambled to his feet. 'I'm going to turn myself in, as they say in the movies. A night in the cells will at least save me from a thank-you tea with Petal Butterkiss.'

'You're not even sorry, are you?' said Annie angrily.

Clingon shrugged. 'They're a couple of good little horses. You tell that twit of a headmaster to hang on to them. They're money-makers, mark my words.'

Annie stood in the lane watching as Clingon approached the police. They talked together for a while, and then Clingon climbed into the police car and disappeared from sight. Annie trailed back towards the school.

From the top of a small hill Brandon and Stephanie were watching.

'I might have known that girl would be involved,' Brandon said grimly.

'How do you know it had anything to do with her?' asked Stephanie.

'I just know,' said Brandon.

Chapter 12

'The show must go on,' Petal had murmured as she came round from her faint, and go on it did. The actors were in fine spirit, believing that after such a disastrous start nothing else could be as bad. Consequently they were not at all nervous when the procession rather raggedly made its way to the school theatre for the performance of 'Scenes from Camelot'.

Petal warned them that she would be appearing unexpectedly on stage to cast a curse upon the house of Arthur; she wouldn't be telling them when this would happen because it was supposed to be a shock when Brusen appeared. So the frightened squeals halfway through the play were absolutely authentic. There was a sudden flash of light (courtesy of Manfred and the Sixth Form Pyrotechnics Club) and the evil Brusen delivered her curse in ringing tones which turned the blood of the audience cold, and inspired the other actors to give their very best performance.

Afterwards, among the milling crowds in the dining-hall where Mrs Barton had adapted several authentic Arthurian recipes given to her by Petal into some wonderful moist cakes and warm, spicy drinks, Annie watched Petal talking to reporters. There were a couple from the national press as well as the local mob, this being a quiet time of the year for big news stories.

'The name of Petal Butterkiss still has pulling power,' said Stephanie at her shoulder.

'It's amazing, isn't it?' said Annie. 'I mean, the whole thing was a disaster out there in the lanes, but now it's been reshaped into a great new dramatic interpretation. You would never be able to tell that, a couple of hours ago, the great Petal Butterkiss was in a dead faint and the whole thing looked set to collapse.'

'Mmm. Or that the school bursar would be reduced to a quivering wreck and have to be led away by an innocent schoolgirl.'

Annie felt herself blush. The slight, sarcastic emphasis on the word 'innocent' told her that Stephanie was beginning to piece things together.

'That stuff about Mr Clingon being overcome with bashful modesty when his gift was discovered was quite superb, Annie,' said Stephanie evenly. 'Now, are you going to tell me what really went on?'

'I . . . don't think I know what you're getting at,' said Annie evasively.

'Oh, I think you do,' said Stephanie. 'But I expect you don't know how much I already know – about Clingon, I mean. Maybe we should compare notes. I'll see you tomorrow, in the art studio, before breakfast. Bring your fellow-conspirators.' Stephanie had seen Annie's parents and Emma and Gayle bearing down upon them, and she moved away before Annie could question her any further.

'That were right grand,' said her father enthusiastically. 'Fancy Petal Butterkiss herself making an appearance. I never thought I'd see such a thing, in all my born days . . .'

'Wow!' said Emma. 'It sure beats the Bradford High Christmas play, I can tell you. We've got a sad carol concert and a Christmas poetry competition.'

'You were very good,' said Gayle.

Annie laughed. 'Thank you. Yes, I thought I moved among the crowd of peasants in a very authentic way. I hope you didn't miss my line. I was one of the people who shouted "God bless King Arthur," you know.'

'It was very well done,' said Emma with a smile. 'You deserved an Oscar. Now, where's the grub? I can smell it, but I can't see it. Lead the way, peasant!'

Annie's mum and dad were soon deep in conversation with some of the other parents, and Annie moved around the hall with Emma and Gayle, taking them to say hello to all her friends and explaining the various things that went on at the school. She was stopped in her tracks by the sight of Natalie, looking so happy she could burst, on the arm of a woman who could only be her mother, they looked so alike. The woman was accompanied by a gentle-looking man with red hair. He was smiling broadly.

'Well, hello,' said Annie, going up to Natalie. 'I wanted you to meet my friends from back home. This is Gayle, and this is Emma.'

'Hello,' said Natalie. 'And these are my people from home. This is my mother, Kathleen Shaugnessy. And this is Michael O'Neill, who is my mother's friend and soon to be my own stepfather.'

'Well!' said Annie, astonished. 'I'm right glad to see you. Natalie thought . . . she thought you might not be able to make it tonight.'

'Nor would I,' said Kathleen with a smile, 'were it not for Michael here. I have been rather adrift, these past few years. I was . . . unwell, you might say, and my head wasn't straight. But Michael made me see that there were things worth fighting for. When I got Natalie's letter, asking me to come, I was in a state . . .'

'Would you believe,' said Natalie, 'that the foul woman who married my father had been telling her all this time that I didn't want to know her . . . and at the same time telling me that my mother didn't care!'

'I wrote to you, Natalie,' said Kathleen, her eyes filling with tears. 'I wrote long letters. But of course, I only knew your home address. They never told me you were away at school . . .'

'She must have ripped up the letters,' said Natalie. 'Well, I'd like to see my father take her side now, when he hears what she's done.'

'There'll be time enough to worry about that tomorrow,' said Michael. 'For now, let's just have a good evening and get to know each other.'

'We're off to the Blue Dolphin for a late supper,' beamed Natalie. 'Maybe we'll see Clingon there, eh? With his shady friend.'

'No, no. Poor Mr Clingon is down at the police station. It will be a long time before he goes to a restaurant again. And serve him right.'

'What *are* you talking about?' asked Emma.

Annie and Natalie smiled at each other. 'I'll tell you later,' said Annie. 'It's a long story – one which will probably take the whole journey home tomorrow to tell. Come on, let's find that food. I'll see you later, Nat.'

It was very late by the time the friends all met up together again. The visitors were all tucked up in the hotel and various guest-houses in surrounding villages, and everyone was tired out by the excitements of the day. But the gang still gathered in the girls' room to share experiences of what had happened. Annie told them that Stephanie wanted to see them the following day, before they all went home.

'She knows something,' said Annie. 'I don't know exactly what. I suppose we'll have to come clean. But unless he's confessed, I still don't know if there'll be enough to convict him. I mean, he did turn himself in, but he's a slippery one. You can't quite make him out. Such a sad, pathetic little man, you think. And then you realise he's simply being devious and trying to get you to feel sorry for him. The police might let him go, if they think he's just a bit nutty.'

'They may well,' said Carin. 'We didn't find what you could call real evidence that he was defrauding the school. In any case, I expect that other man was the real brains behind it all, and we have no proof of ever seeing him, or any knowledge of how he might be found. Clingon could still get away with it by saying that the horses were a long-term investment, and he always meant the school to have every penny. I bet he's got proper accounts. I doubt the police will be able to do very much, anyway. It's all circumstantial.'

'It will make it very hard for him to do anything else, though,' said Annie. 'I mean, he's not stupid. He'll know that someone's keeping an eye on him. And I don't suppose we'll be the only ones asking questions about where he gets enough money to be so involved in racing. At least his little business empire is coming to an end, as far as King Arthur's is concerned.'

A knock at the door startled them. It was a sixth former, bearing an envelope. Inside was a message from the headmaster: all six of them were to appear in his study at nine o'clock the following morning: *This meeting is in place of your arrangement to see Miss Stephanie Harvey in the art studio. Please make sure you are on time.*

It was signed by the headmaster.

'Whoops!' said Lance.

'Do you think we'll be expelled?' asked Sonja nervously.

'For what? For exposing a fraud by the school bursar?' said Annie.

'No, for committing our own fraud by impersonating him and putting his valuable horses at risk, not to mention the damage to the reputation of the school,' said Carin quietly. 'It could look very bad for us, if we haven't got good evidence against Clingon.'

'I see what you mean. Make Clingon into an innocent man who just happens to have enough private wealth to support a couple of racehorses, and we're the criminal ones,' said Annie miserably.

'There is no point in worrying about it now,' said Sonja. 'Tomorrow we will all be going far away, so the fuss can die down over Christmas. By the New Year, perhaps things will look better, and everyone will have calmed down.'

They all murmured agreement, though not very convincingly. Finally, at around two o'clock in the morning, they all went to their own beds, to get what sleep they could amidst the anxieties about the meeting with the headmaster.

Annie prepared many stories to tell about how exactly they got the information about the horses without doing anything so criminal as breaking into Clingon's private office and going through his personal belongings. None of them sounded at all convincing.

At nine o'clock promptly the next morning they gathered outside the study and the grim-faced secretary showed them in. Mr Asquith was seated at his desk. There were two uniformed police officers with him, and a man in a suit. Stephanie was there, too.

'Allow me to introduce everyone,' said Charles gravely. He named the teenagers standing in front of him, and then told them that Police Constables Jones and Whitworth would be taking statements from them in due course.

'And this is Chief Inspector Henry, who wishes to hear

everything you know about these racehorses, and about Mr Clingon.'

The friends stood in a row, silent. No one knew what to say.

Charles looked at Annie. 'I think we'll start with you, Annie,' he said. 'I have a feeling that this pageant stunt might have been your idea?'

Annie started to stumble through the account of how they had met Clingon and another man in the garden, and how they had become suspicious when they saw them again at the Blue Dolphin.

The others chipped in now and again when she forgot something, or to add a comment of their own. Lance, of course, said nothing. He simply waved his hair in agreement from time to time.

Chief Inspector Henry listened very attentively, and the police officers made notes in their notebooks. When Annie had finished, the Chief Inspector asked her, 'Why on earth didn't you come to us with your suspicions about Mr Clingon right at the beginning?'

'I don't think you would have believed us,' said Annie. 'After all, the only stuff we had was a conversation in the garden, which they explained by saying the weather was too nice to work indoors, and another meeting at the Blue Dolphin. We're only kids, aren't we? I thought we could get Clingon to give back what he'd taken once he knew he was rumbled. But more than that was unlikely. If we came and told you we'd seen some account sheets that didn't make sense to us, and seen two people talking in a way that made us suspicious, are you really telling me you'd have taken us seriously?'

'I see your point,' said DCI Henry. 'But what you didn't know was how much we already knew about this case. Your evidence would have been very helpful, if we'd had it. Instead, you went for this elaborate charade. It could have gone very badly wrong . . .'

'Could have?' Natalie picked up on the words and the slight smile which accompanied them.

'Fortunately for you,' said Stephanie, 'I had my own suspicions about Mr Clingon, some time ago. I have been in touch with the police, and we were together collecting the evidence we needed to get him properly, using the proper channels. He was being watched. You lot blundered into a very careful police operation. Clingon was not the only one we had an eye on. Actually, he was a bit out of his league in this particular caper. Clingon was a small fish in a big pond, playing at being one of the real villains. We were hoping to make several arrests after Christmas, on the basis of information painstakingly gathered over the last eighteen months.'

'We didn't know about the racehorses,' said DCI Henry, 'but we knew about other things. We were hoping to get the big names at the top of the sorry little tree of corruption. You put all that at risk, with your daft escapade. We'll get Clingon, for sure, but I don't know about the others we have our eye on. Not now.'

'I'm really sorry,' said Annie. 'We had no idea. No idea at all. Does this mean you can't prove anything?'

'Mr Clingon is being interviewed as we speak,' said DCI Henry. 'He indicated last night that he wanted to make a clean breast of it. So, we'll see.'

'Quite so,' said Charles. 'Now, in view of the fact that there is an ongoing police investigation in which no doubt you will have to be involved, I have decided not to take any action about your behaviour myself. I do wish you all to know, however, that I am very disappointed and not a little irritated by your arrogance in assuming you could take on such a man without harm to the investigation, to yourselves, to others and to the school. Any number of people could have been put at risk by the way you behaved. You had no idea what you were taking on, and you blundered in without thought. I will be watching you all quite carefully over the next few terms. Please do not allow yourselves to believe that wealth and status – even royal status,' he added, looking at Uem, 'mean you can do as you please. Now I think you had better go and pack your things.' He raised his hand as they turned to leave. 'One more thing before you go. Next term I expect to see a huge improvement in attitude. Also, since you clearly have too much spare time on your hands, I expect to see more involvement with out-of-lessons activities. To make a start, I have enrolled you in one of my wife's lunch-time positive thinking groups . . .'

He nodded briefly to dismiss them, and watched them go with a quiet smile.

'Please, just send me to prison,' said Sonja, when they were safely outside. 'Anything rather than one of Petal's groups.'

'At least it's only one for you,' said Carin. 'Don't forget I've already had four sessions. Believe me, that's enough to stretch anyone's endurance. What do you think this will do to me?'

'Ooh, he's a smooth operator,' groaned Annie. 'I under-estimated him. He is just like a real headmaster after all. Our lives will be hell next term.'

'He has insisted upon me removing my Neru from the premises also,' said Uem. 'Manfred took him away last night to Mr Plumberry, and this morning a note was delivered to my room which told me I must pay for his accommodation at the surgery and visit him there. He is not to enter school grounds on any account. I asked Manfred to arrange a bribe for the headmaster, but Manfred would not do it. He said it would not work.'

'Just as well you asked Manfred first,' said Annie. 'I have a feeling you really would have been out on your ear if you had tried to bribe the headmaster. Still, it's not far to Plumberry's, Uem. Neru will be happy there – and Mr Plumberry will be more than happy to have him.'

'His wife won't,' grinned Carin.

'Well, I suppose this is it,' said Annie, 'the end of our first term at King Arthur's. My mum and dad are picking me up in about ten minutes' time, to go home. Where are you going, Natalie? I can tell by that smile it's not Switzerland with the Ice Maiden!'

'I am going home to Dublin for Christmas,' said Natalie. 'And my father is coming – without the Ice Maiden – in the New Year. He and my mother have an appointment with a lawyer in Dublin. Things will get sorted out so that I can spend time with my mum and with my dad.'

'What about the Ice Maiden?' asked Carin. 'What will happen to her?'

Natalie shrugged. 'Nothing, I suppose. My dad loves her, he'll forgive her. But he'll be a bit less willing to believe everything she says, maybe. Anyway, I don't care. I'll have somewhere else to go, won't I, when she gets too much.'

'Next term, Natalie,' said Annie firmly, 'we shall apply our minds to your battles with the Ice Maiden. You're not on your own any more.'

'This has all worked out in splendicacious fashion,' beamed Uem. 'By this time tomorrow, we will all be reunited with our precocious families wherever they are in the world – in my case, I will also be WARM! We will have a wonderful festival, and return from our beloved families to our beloved friends. It is good to have such balance in one's life, is it not?'

'Yes, it is,' agreed Annie warmly. She was really looking forward to spending time at home with her parents over

Christmas. It would be great to hang out with Gayle and Emma again. But coming back to boarding-school would not be quite as dismal as she had feared at the beginning of the term, when she had arrived on the station platform among a crowd of strangers, feeling unsure of herself and desperately homesick. King Arthur's English Academy had its very own Hollywood film star, Lunatic Lord and resident criminal. Not many schools could boast those among their facilities. It was perhaps not quite what her parents had planned for her education. But perhaps she could survive it all the same. She already had a couple of ideas hatching for next term.

Natalie, for instance – it was time she stood up to her stepmother, who had do ne what Annie considered to be the unforgivable. She was sure the six brains put together could come up with a suitable plan to pay her back. Then there was the romance between Manfred and Nurse Guptah. That didn't seem to be progressing very far. They could do with a bit of a helping hand.

'Cheers then,' Annie said to her friends, raising her can of Coke to theirs. 'Have a great Christmas, and we'll see each other again next year. I propose a toast: to the Lunatic Lord and his crazy academy. May school life never be dull and boring again.'

Also available from Piccadilly Press:

HELP! MY SOCIAL LIFE IS A MESS!
A Survival Guide For Teenagers

Kathryn Lamb

Is your social life non-existent? Ruined by friends you don't like? Interrupted by school and homework? Or just in need of a bit of recuperation?

See how Basil Broke, Soumik Sen, Amy Average, Angelica Toogood and Steve Cash improve *their* lousy social lives in this essential guide.

But remember . . . Your idea of what your social life should be (the party scene, fantastic boy/girlfriend, fun! fun! fun!, forget to sleep, don't worry Mum/Dad, I'll be back by 4a.m.) may differ in some respects from your parents' idea.

So don't worry a parent. A worried parent is a problem parent, a parent who likes to say "No!"

Also available from Piccadilly Press:

ENTER THE BOY-ZONE
Sport Sorted for Girls

Caroline Plaisted

Do you know your 'scrim' from your 'scrum', or a 'lob' from an 'LBW'? Have you ever wondered what goes on in that strange world that boys inhabit – the world of sport? Here are all the details you need for a working knowledge of many kinds of sports and, more importantly, the low-down on the sportsmen worth watching.

Football, cricket, Rugby, Grand Prix . . . you'll be able to bluff your way impressively in all kinds of sports.